Eastside School 1873-1917

Mulberry School, 1918-2003

Other Books by Eric T. Reynolds

Novels:
The Artifacts: A Flint Hills Story
The Road to Sugar Loaf: A Suffragist's Story

Anthologies edited:
   Golden Age SF: Tales of a Bygone Future
   Visual Journeys: A Tribute to Space Artists
   Return to Luna (with the National Space Society)
   Desolate Places
   Barren Worlds
   Destination: Future (Co-edited with Z.S. Adani)
   Footprints (Co-edited with Jay Lake)
   Origins
   World Jumping
   The Ruins anthology series:
   Ruins Terra
   Ruins Extraterrestrial
   Ruins Excavation

The Legend of Mulberry School

The Legend of Mulberry School

A Paranormal Historical Novel

Eric T. Reynolds

HADLEY RILLE BOOKS

Cover Design © Hadley Rille Books
Cover Photography:
Mulberry School © Hadley Rille Books
Author Photo © 2022 Eric T. Reynolds
Building Photos © Eric T. Reynolds

ISBN-13 978-1-7350938-5-7

Trade paperback edition

Other editions Available:
Hardcover
Ebook
Audiobook
Edited by Rose Reynolds, Laura Ripper & Nancy Reynolds
v2.0
Published in the United States of America, and worldwide by
Hadley Rille Books
Kansas City, USA
www.hrbpress.com
contact@hadleyrillebooks.com

To all Teachers past, present, and future

1917

Prologue

Eastside School, Eureka, Kansas

On February 16, 1917, the stately stone building on Mulberry Street known as Eastside Grade School burned to the ground. Citizens were quick to approve a bond sale for building a new school at the same location.

Construction on Mulberry School began on June 10th of that year. The contractor promised:

"The work will be pushed as rapidly as possible. It is hoped to have the building ready for occupancy by January First."

They reused some of Eastside's original foundation stones for Mulberry School on the new school's east side.

* * *

Months after starting, on a mild, sunny September 10th, morning, a breeze whipped around the southeast corner of the Mulberry School's foundation. Marcus sat there with a tray of mortar and a trowel, touching up the grout lines. Everyone hoped the new schoolhouse would last well over 100 years; Marcus hoped his children and grandchildren and their children would attend someday.

He wanted to make sure the building would never fail on account of his work. But the fate of Eastside School proved that long building life isn't guaranteed.

Marcus finished up and got ready to leave. Running his fingers across the rough surface, the stone seemed to fade into his imagination conveying the significance of these corner stones as they presented a continuity with that ill-fated first schoolhouse that had stood here since 1873.

Five months later, an accident claimed the life of a carpenter, a month before Mulberry School's dedication.

January 4, 1918

Six weeks before

"Your students should be glad to move into the new school," said Rose as she and Maggie strolled along the courthouse block toward Oxford Rooming Home on North Main Street.

"They can't wait," said Maggie. "We've had enough of that high school attic. They'll have lots to say when classes resume."

The two women halted at the honk of a puttering Model T and the clomping of a horse and buggy as the car swerved to avoid a collision.

"That was close," said Rose, turning to Maggie, who was now gazing toward the courthouse grounds.

"Ready? Let's go," said Rose.

"Who is that?" asked Maggie, referring to a man standing on the courthouse lawn, looking up at the spires of the ornate building.

"He's new in town. I don't know anything about him."

"What do you suppose he's looking at?"

"Why don't you go ask him?"

"I don't think I should."

"Actually," said Rose, "I have seen him around town a little, probably learning about Eureka."

"Well," said Maggie, "I'm a bit tired; let's sit on the bench next to the gazebo."

"Tired? Already?"

"Let's go," Maggie said, taking Rose's hand, "before I'm not tired anymore."

They went over to the gazebo area and settled onto the bench.

"Phew!" said Maggie.

"Oh, sure."

"I just want a better look without being obvious."

"We're obvious anyway," said Rose.

"All right," said Maggie, "switch places with me so it'll appear I'm talking to you instead of looking his direction."

Rose laughed. "Right. Let's not be obvious."

"He's intrigued by that building."

"He's going to notice us watching him," said Rose. "Are you ready to go yet?"

"No. I'm still a bit tired," said Maggie. "You go on. I'll meet you later."

Maggie pulled an old letter from her bag and pretended to read it. After a minute or two, the man walked behind the courthouse. Maggie put the letter away and got ready to go home. As she stood, the man emerged from the other side and stopped again to look up at the building. He then appeared to be heading to the post office.

Maggie rushed to the sidewalk and hurried toward the Oxford, catching up to Rose.

"Well, you got your energy back, didn't you?" said Rose.

"I just remembered I have things to mail."

* * *

A few minutes later.

"Excuse me, sir," Maggie said to the man ahead of her chatting with the teller. "Will you be long?"

He turned around and smiled.

Maggie felt a sudden warmth inside when their eyes met.

"Why no, miss," he said, running his fingers through his black hair. "I'm finished."

Maggie felt herself blushing. "I'm sorry. I'm in a bit of a hurry."

"That's all right," he said, stepping aside as he quickly gathered his envelopes.

He moved too fast and tripped, tossing his envelopes to the floor, bumping into Maggie, knocking her over.

"Oh! I'm so sorry," he said, diving to the floor to gather up her packages and his envelopes.

Maggie started to get on her hands and knees to help. Their eyes met again when she reached for a far envelope.

They both stood and faced each other, Maggie chuckling with her fingertips flat against her mouth. "Are you all right?" she said, still giggling.

"Yes," he said, handing her packages to her. "Please excuse my clumsiness. Did I ruin any of your packages?"

She shuffled them in her arms, still laughing. "No, sir, there's nothing breakable in them." She straightened up. "Well," she said. "You remind me of my late father. His clumsiness was amusing." She then regretted saying that.

"I'm honored," he said, straightening his envelopes, managing to keep them together.

"Are you new here?" she asked as she stepped to the teller window.

"Yes. I just moved here from El Dorado, and I'm just getting settled in."

She finished her task with the teller quickly turned and said, "Well, welcome to Eureka. My name is Maggie Stilwell."

"Glad to know you, Miss Stilwell. I am Ricky Austin," he said, offering his hand.

She took his hand and shook it. "And you, Mr. Austin."

"Nice to have some warmer weather, today," he said, managing a feeble smile with his attempt at small talk.

"Yes, it is," she said. "Have you found a place to live? The rooming houses are filling up."

"Yes. I found a place on Main Street just in time. I'll be trying for a job to work with Mueller Construction that's building the new grade school."

"Well," she said, "I'll be teaching Eighth Grade English there when it's ready for us."

"I hope you'll all enjoy your new building. It should be ready by April, barring any problems." He started fidgeting and diverted his gaze.

"I'm looking forward to moving there as are my students," she said. "We're stuck in the high school attic until then. April's a little later than the original January First date we hoped for."

"They had delays, I think, because of weather. I'll probably find out more when I start work. I'm glad you're getting a new school."

"Thank you, Mr. Austin."

Well," he said, looking toward the exit. "I must be going. Again, glad to meet you, Miss Stilwell."

"Ta-ta. Good luck with the job," she said.

"Thank you," he said as he left.

She sorted through her envelopes, adjusted her coat and went to the door. When she stepped outside, he was already on Third Street, crossing Oak Street toward the courthouse. It would have been nice, she thought, if he offered to walk with her. She sighed and started to head over to Third Street herself.

* * *

As Ricky walked around the courthouse, he wanted to slap himself. "I was a complete fool," he muttered. "She is nice. I wish I could get to know her." He tapped his chest. "That was a nice feeling inside when our eyes met."

He stopped, looked up at the ornate building, and considered its architecture, an interest of his.

"French Renaissance," he said aloud, then continued to the corner of Third and Main Streets and found a bench in front of the Greenwood Hotel. Since it was warmer today, he decided to sit and open a letter of particular interest among the forwarded mail from his previous home in El Dorado.

He read through the letter twice. It appeared he would be staying in Eureka for a while. The Selective service rejected him because of a "physical deficiency." His upper body strength and coordination were considered inferior.

He sighed and put the letter away. He wasn't sure he wanted to go to war anyway—like many men wanted to—and he accepted the verdict without further thought. It seemed to him that he failed twice this day: clumsiness in front of a nice young woman and being rejected because of a physical deficiency. A blow to his manhood.

"Manhood, whatever," he mumbled. "Looks like I can pursue my other plans now."

He gazed around downtown and got ready to get up and leave, but Miss Stilwell was walking along the sidewalk toward him so he figured he'd stay and watch her walk by.

"Hello there," she said as she passed by him.

"Hello," he managed to blurt out.

Later that afternoon

"You tripped over your own two feet and knocked her down right there in the post office?" Benny said. He sat back on the rooming house porch chair and kicked his legs out during a small burst of laughter. "And it was Maggie Stilwell?"

"Yes," Ricky said. "She's a teacher."

"You're lucky she's the one you made a fool of yourself in front of. Some might have thought of you as rude."

"I'm impressed with her," Ricky said. "So nice, and I think she's quite attractive. And, you know? I think she did kind of like me."

Benny slapped him on the shoulder. "That's right. Stay positive."

"I try to," Ricky said. "I'd like to get up the nerve to talk to her, maybe ask her to meet for coffee."

"Then go ahead. And by the way, I put in a good word for you at Mueller Construction. I think you'll get in. Mr. Stanchfield said it'll be a month or so to take you on. You'll do all right. The work isn't hard."

That Evening

In the Oxford Rooming Home, Maggie sat in the living room chatting about the day with her friend Annie Marsh.

"You feel that way about him after a short meeting like that?" Annie said.

"His bumbling shyness was precious. He was genuine and nice. And not that it's important, but he's kind of handsome."

"Sounds like love at first sight," said Annie.

"Well, he's intriguing," said Maggie.

"I think I've seen him. He's been out around town, getting familiar with it."

"I hope I see him around more."

Annie stood to leave. "I hope you do, too."

"Thanks for coming by," said Maggie.

"Of course. I'll come by tomorrow, too. I'm headed to see Marcus now. He's just a couple of buildings down."

January 25, 1918

Three Weeks before

When classes were finished for the day, Maggie headed out of the high school and walked to downtown. She reached Main Street and noticed how the unseasonably warm weather seemed to be lifting everyone's general mood. She turned south on Main Street to visit a store before five-o'clock closing. Along the way, her mind turned to that nice gentleman, Mr. Austin, she had met in the post office. Halfway to Third Street, she noticed him standing on the courthouse grounds gazing up at the courthouse.

She wondered.

Should I go talk to him? Perhaps he's busy. She wanted to get to know him, but he wasn't showing any intention of approaching her to ask to court her or even invite her to an event or to have coffee. Was he interested? That encounter a few weeks before was special, or was she imagining it was? Who knew?

Do I need to make it obvious that I'm interested? Or I could ask Rose to go to him and tell him my thoughts? No, that's what my junior high students do. I could watch where he usually goes, wait for him and "accidently" bump into him: "Oh, excuse me, Mr. Austin. How clumsy of me. Please help me up?"

Too obvious.

What do other women do? Well, I can't just throw myself at him like Doris would. Even if it gets her noticed, any man would just laugh at me if I did that.

She strolled past a garage that had a Model T inside, idling with smoke pouring out the tailpipe. The old car sounded like it was on its last leg, shaking as if asking for help. Several mechanics tended to it. She walked on past the Princess Theatre and glanced back over at the courthouse. Mr. Austin was still there, staring up at the building, fascinated by something; he looked over at her, smiled and waved. Well! she thought. She returned the smile and wave.

Maybe if we would happen to meet at a town hall meeting, church, or parade celebration, I'd have an excuse to talk to him, assuming other women didn't get to him first.

She walked on toward Frank H. Brooks Clothing Store a couple of blocks down. It looked like Rose and Annie were out front getting ready to enter, so Maggie hurried on.

Inside the store, Maggie approached Annie who was browsing at a rack.

"Maggie!" said Annie. "How are you? Good sale prices today."

"I didn't know," said Maggie.

"Unadvertised. Rose found something right away and she's already trying it on."

Maggie began browsing herself, starting with the coats and scarves.

Annie rejoined her. "Say, are you making progress getting that guy's attention?"

"You mean Mr. Austin?" Maggie said. "A little. I wish I could just go up to him and say, 'Hey Ricky, when are you going to call on me?'"

Annie laughed. "I'm sorry. I don't mean to make light of it. I don't think he's one who would mind if you did, but it might take some doing for him to get the picture."

Rose came from the dressing room and joined them.
"Hello, Maggie," said Rose.

"We were talking about Ricky," said Annie.

"Oh yes, Maggie," said Rose. "What's the latest on Mr. Mysterious?"

"I seem to be catching his eye sometimes when I'm out and about."

"If you were to run into him at an event," said Rose.

"I thought of that, too," said Maggie. "But which?"

"The Senior Class play is in a couple of weeks," suggested Annie. "They're performing *Green Stockings* at the Princess Theatre. Let's go. Maybe he'll show up."

"Maybe," said Maggie.

"Marcus and I will be going," said Annie, "He knows Ricky. I'll tell him to invite that 'new guy' to go with us."

"Won't that be obvious?" asked Maggie.

"Let it be obvious. You're not asking him so what of it?"

* * *

That same afternoon, Ricky decided to make use of his time before he started work in three weeks. A nice day like today was a good opportunity to walk around and get to know the town more, so he set out from his rooming home and did some window shopping. He went down to the Opera House block and as he looked around, he started thinking about that woman, Maggie. She seemed so nice—if only he could get up the nerve to talk to her. Would she say no to any invitation to join him for anything? He didn't know. He stopped to look in Frank H. Brooks at suits, and then went up a couple of blocks to Beardsley-Brown Clothing and looked in the window. They were having a big sale until mid-February, but he didn't want to spend the money, until after he started work. He went across the street to the courthouse lawn and was about to go in the gazebo, but a couple was occupying it. He wandered away and stopped to study the ornate courthouse architecture. After a while, he thought of moving on, but noticed Maggie across the street. She looked in his direction. He smiled and waved. She smiled and waved back.

She walked on, and Ricky thought about her: *Why didn't I call over to her? Why didn't I go over and talk to her?* He felt a knot in his stomach. There she went, on down Main Street. It wouldn't seem right if he ran after her. Chasing her down wouldn't do. Next time he had an opportunity, he needed to approach her in a polite way. He wandered around more and practiced.

"How do you do, Miss Stilwell? I've noticed you walking here sometimes."

No, that's no good.

In a deep voice. "Hello, miss, may I walk you to wherever you're going? Not that you have to tell me. I know it's none of my business."

No. Let's see. "Hi there, Maggie. How in the world are you—are you busy?"

No. How do other guys do it? It's the wrong time of year to wear a short sleeve shirt to show off my muscles, except I don't have muscles like some guys, like Benny and Marcus and others. Maybe I'm not worthy of her or any woman. But she looks at me often. Should I splurge and get a new suit with my oil rig money I saved up?

Maybe I'll keep an eye on her and get all dressed up and go lean against the Greenwood Hotel and wait until she passes by, then wink at her and say, "Well, hello, good-lookin'."

But I won't feel comfortable doing that. My voice would squeak and I'd look like a fool. There should be another way I can approach her. I have to think up a way.

February 15, 1918

Three days before

Seats were filling up fast in the Princess Theatre auditorium for the performance of *Green Stockings*. Maggie found herself glancing back toward the entrance at times. She, Annie, and Marcus were in their seats toward the left of their row. Annie leaned across the empty seat between Maggie and her. "I think he'll be here," she said, patting the vacant chair.

"Is this obvious, saving this seat for him right next to me?" said Maggie, looking around again.

"Marcus doesn't want to block the lady's view from behind this seat with him being tall. How tall is Ricky?"

"About average, I think," said Maggie.

Things started quieting down; Maggie looked around and didn't see Ricky yet.

"You'd better go back there and meet him at the door," Annie said to Marcus.

He got up and went to the entrance. Moments later, he and Ricky reached their row. Marcus pointed to the seat between Maggie and Annie. "That one," he said.

Ricky, looking sharp in his suit, smiled and nodded. His foot bumped a seat in the row in front of them as he squeezed past Annie to take the seat next to Maggie.

He sat. "Hello," he said to Maggie, offering his hand. "Remember the post office? I almost did it again sliding over here."

She shook his hand. "Well, I'm glad you didn't," she said, as he sat down. She immediately wished she hadn't said that. Then, "Nice to see you tonight."

"Likewise," he said. He started to lean over to say something else, but the lights dimmed and the curtain opened.

*　*　*

At the end of Act One, Ricky leaned over to Maggie and said, "This is exceedingly well portrayed."

"And that Catherine Coulter is playing the Celia part so well," Maggie said.

As the curtain opened for Act Two, Maggie felt anxious wondering what Ricky was about to say just before the beginning of Act One. She tried not to think about it during the next two acts. The play was so good, she just enjoyed it. After the final curtain, the four of them went to the lobby and stood among people milling around.

"I don't think I'll ever stop laughing," said Annie.

"You never stop laughing," teased Marcus.

Maggie laughed. "That is so true," she said.

Ricky chuckled with them but didn't say anything.

"Well," said Marcus, "shall we walk the ladies home? Miss Stilwell, you live at the Oxford, don't you? Ricky's and my rooming house is close by there. I'll walk Annie home and you could accompany Miss Stilwell to her home if you would, Ricky."

"My pleasure," Ricky said.

He and Maggie walked up Main Street to the Oxford, mostly making small talk and acting in a formal manner along the way.

When they reached their rooming houses' block and approached the Oxford, Ricky said, "That was an enjoyable evening, Miss Stilwell."

"It certainly was," she said, "but may call me Maggie."

"I enjoyed this evening, Maggie," he said, "And please call me Ricky. As such, I was going to ask. . ."

"Yes?"

A minute later, they reached the Oxford's front porch. "Good night, Maggie," he said. "Thank you for the nice company."

"Good night, Ricky," she said.

February 18, 1918

Maggie

The day of the accident

On one of the last days before her class moved into the new school, Maggie started out early from the Oxford Rooming House and paused on the sidewalk out front to check her timing. She gazed down to another rooming house a few buildings ahead. Ricky was on the porch settled on a chair with his coffee, so she pinched her cheeks and started along the sidewalk. When she passed by his porch, her eyes met his; she smiled and waved, wiggling her fingers. Ricky waved back, returning the smile, then his housemate Benny emerged from the front door. She gave him a polite smile and continued on.

She was anxious to know what it was he was going to say last Friday evening and hoped she would find out tonight after both were home.

Several blocks later, she glanced back and noticed Ricky and Benny stepping off the porch to go to the construction site.

She reached Fourth Street and turned toward the direction of the high school, pulling her coat and scarf tightly against the slight chill as she walked on toward the school. She reached Mulberry Street and paused for a moment. She loved to gaze at the beautiful houses on the corners here, most of which she didn't think she'd ever

29

be able to afford, but she had to get going. As she crossed the street, she wondered how Ricky was doing at his new job just a couple of blocks south of here. It would be nice if he would show her more interest, but she didn't know what to try. He noticed her whenever she walked by his rooming house. Perhaps she'd think of something.

She went on to Maple Street and gazed at the houses ahead, then she felt a sudden wave of affection for Ricky, filling her with a warm feeling—perhaps it *was* love at first sight.

But time flew by, so she hurried and reached the wide sidewalk at the high school's entrance, got to the main floor, and stopped in the teachers' lounge.

George Fielding stood when she entered the room. "Good morning, Miss Stilwell," he said, pointing to a side table. "Fresh coffee."

"Thank you, Mr. Fielding. Any news here?"

"Nothing I know," he said. "Although, Principal Fuller was just called away."

"Oh?" Maggie frowned. "That's odd at this time of day. Called away for what?"

"I don't know," he said. "It was rather abrupt."

She glanced at the clock. "Well then, I'll get on up to my class. Have a good day, Mr. Fielding." She hung up her coat, clutched her purse and started to leave.

"Have another good day in the penthouse," he said.

She hopped up the stairs to her makeshift classroom. Some of her students were there, ready for class.

"We'll wait for the others as it's still a bit early."

After more students entered, she said, "Well, you'll all soon be in the new school. We'll move over in a couple of weeks. The workmen will still be finishing some of the rooms, but we're being allowed to move in early!"

Her students applauded.

"It'll finally be nice to move in after the construction delays, won't it?"

More applause.

One student raised her hand. "Miss Stilwell? What will our classes be like?"

"Well, my English classroom will be on the second floor over on the west side. The classrooms are quite modern. The other junior high classes will be on that floor, too. Of course, you all will be back in this building next year."

Their happy expressions fell.

"But," Maggie continued, "you'll be in real classrooms again after you graduate from junior high this May."

Applause, once more.

"All right," she said, "let's get started." As she went to the chalkboard, Violette from Principal Fuller's office emerged from the stairs and knocked lightly on a wood beam. Maggie nodded at her, and she approached Maggie to whisper something.

"Miss Fuller needs to see you down in her office at once."

"That's unusual she'd need to see me," said Maggie.

She gave her students a page number in their classics book to start reading and excused herself to follow Violette down to Principal Fuller's office.

Harriet Fuller sat behind her desk and sighed. George Fielding was there, along with several other teachers.

"Have a seat, please," Fuller said to Maggie. "Now everyone, there's been an accident at the Mulberry School construction site and they're looking for friends or relatives of the victim. The sheriff reports that Ricky Austin fell from scaffolding about twenty minutes ago and has died."

Maggie drew her hands to her face. "Oh!"

"If any of you know someone who's related to Mr. Austin or knows him, please let me know and I'll arrange to pass that along to the Greenwood County Sheriff's department. They'll contact anyone who's associated with him."

Maggie didn't say anything for a moment.

"It's a shock I know," Fuller said. She noticed Maggie's expression. "Miss Stilwell, did you know Mr. Austin?"

"Yes," replied Maggie. "He was a friend."

"I think it's all right if you take the rest of the day off, if you need to."

Maggie went home around 9:30 after she informed her students of the tragedy. When she reached Main Street and walked by Ricky's rooming house, she didn't know what to think. It was as if her emotions had been stripped away. She kept walking around and started talking out loud.

"I can't believe it," she said aloud. "I just saw him full of life!"

February 18, 1918

Ricky

The day of the accident

Ricky sat with his cup of coffee on the small rooming house porch during a chilly morning watching Main Street just like every morning and thought about the upcoming day. Hammering from the new, larger Charles Stith rooming house being built nearby echoed around the area. He thought about the new school and wasn't sure what to expect at his new job there today, but he figured it'd be less hazardous than being an oil field worker after that close call on the rig a month before. It was a good job, but not one he was well-suited to do. His boss must have felt the same, since he didn't care if Ricky left on short notice. "With this glut of willing workers, I'll have three new men on board this week," he had said.

Maggie Stilwell passed by along the sidewalk, interrupting Ricky's thoughts. She smiled and waved, wiggling her fingers this time. She often walked by early. When Ricky told Benny a couple of days before about her walking by, he had said, "Of course she does. You're so naïve you wouldn't know she likes you even if she came up and told you."

Ricky smiled at her and waved back.

The door opened behind him and Benny stepped out.

"I'm the best-looking guy in town, yet she prefers you," Benny said.

Ricky shrugged. "If you say so."

"No matter, though," Benny said. "You ready for today? Don't worry, you'll be thanking me by tonight for getting you this job. I'll let you buy me lunch on Saturday."

"Yeah. Guess it's time to go soon," Ricky said.

A few minutes later, they headed to the sidewalk and went down Main Street, and when they reached Third Street, they stopped for a moment on the corner in front of the Greenwood Hotel. Ricky checked his watch.

Benny pointed up Main Street. "There's Maggie. She's starting out to the high school now that she's finished her morning errand." He nudged Ricky with his elbow, causing him to stumble a little.

"Lay off, Benny," Ricky said, regaining his balance. "She's a nice girl. I like watching her walk by."

"If she's sweet on you, maybe you shouldn't get to know her so she doesn't know what you're really like."

Ricky laughed and punched Benny in the arm. "Not bad for a guy who's not the best-looking in town, right?"

Benny put his hand on Ricky's shoulder. "Look up, chum, you'll get more handsome when you get a few more years on you, and maybe you'll grow up and have the courage to talk to her, but you'll lose the chance if you don't act fast."

They walked along East Third, leaving the hotel behind and passed by A.C. Houston Lumber Company, where they stopped for a moment, looking in at the stacks of lumber on the main grounds behind a fence.

"Love that smell," Benny said. "But come on, let's go."

They walked uphill toward Mulberry Street and when they reached it, Ricky pointed to house styles he liked.

"There's a nice bungalow," he said, pointing to the left on Mulberry Street. "And what I call a cross between Edwardian and Victorian," he said, gesturing to the big house on the corner.

"You should study to be an architect," Benny said.

"I plan to. Maybe this job could be a start."

"Could be. We're close to finishing the school. Do well and you might get another job like this."

"Hope so," Ricky said.

"Eastside School stood for forty-five years. I went through grade school there. That was so sad when it burned last year."

"I went there, too," Ricky said. "Although I'm from El Dorado, we did live here for a couple of years and I went to Eastside for fourth and fifth grades. A lot of memories there."

When they reached the site, Ricky was supposed to meet Bart Stanchfield in the front entrance area. They entered the large brick building through the front doors. Ricky assumed Stanchfield was the man in bib overalls surrounded by workers next to some scaffolding in the middle of the cavernous entryway.

"You're Ricky?" he asked.

Ricky tried not to sound anxious. "Yes, sir. I'm ready to work."

"Of course you are," he said. "Are you sure you can do this kind of work?" Stanchfield looked him up and down.

Ricky nodded. "Whatever you need me to do."

"Let's get started," Stanchfield said.

"Mr. Stanchfield?" Ricky said, "it looks like the schoolhouse is nearly complete. What's left?"

Stanchfield gestured above the scaffolding. "We have some work on the ceiling to finish up."

The scaffolding had a ladder propped against the lowest of three bound-wood plank platforms, each suspended by cables from the one above it. A ladder from each angled up to the next, to the upper platform.

"We need to secure that light fixture," he said, pointing to a white globe suspended from a freshly varnished crossbeam. He then pointed to a worker nearby. "This is Cheney. He has your tools and he's in charge of this area."

Ricky looked up and around at the upper scaffolding. It was high up there. He didn't know he would have to climb up high.

Stanchfield interrupted his gaze. "Get a-going, boy. We're on a schedule. Mr. Mueller wants this part done today." He shook his head and stepped away.

Cheney turned toward Ricky and chuckled. "Welcome to the Cranky Monday Stanchfield Club on your first day here."

Ricky nodded.

Cheney handed Ricky a tool belt "Well, better get to it. Don't make today your last day."

Ricky secured the tool belt and tried not to think about the ascent as he started up the ladder. It felt secure, but even the first platform looked high. He managed, but was no more comfortable when he reached the first platform. Now he had to scale this next ladder. His foot didn't want to move to the first rung. He finally planted it while holding tight onto the ladder with his white-knuckled hands.

He was taking too long. "Get to it, kid!" Stanchfield called from below.

When Ricky took a couple of deep breaths, the others below started laughing. That actually helped because he was angry that they didn't understand, so he hung on and placed his other foot onto the next rung. He entered a rhythm of breathe-step-pull up, breathe-step-pull up and in half a minute, his hands reached the next platform where he grabbed the plank and tried to lift his foot up to the next rung to get into position, but once he was there, he panicked when his shaking foot swung out into empty air, but he managed a shaky ascent up to the highest platform.

They always say don't look down when you're climbing up high. That's true, but looking up to where he had to climb was worse, because the ceiling was unnaturally close over his head. Ricky couldn't cope with that. He tried not to give in to the urge to glance up, but couldn't keep his eyes from darting. The ceiling right there was like an inverted floor messing with his orientation. Three deep breaths and he pictured Maggie walking by his porch, her friendly face, and how he should have been trying to court her. And then he thought: *If I were only three feet above the floor, I could hold onto the ladder can swing my legs out like an acrobat. I'm strong enough to do it.*

But the thought of empty air all around jabbed into his thoughts that he *wasn't* three feet up. If he missed, he'd fall more than two schoolhouse stories to a hard floor.

No. He couldn't continue. He stepped down a rung and then another.

"All right, boy!" Stanchfield yelled from below. "You're not going to work out here like this. Come down and go home." He mumbled something and the other guys laughed.

Ricky was glad he didn't have to go up more, but now he still had to climb down which could be worse and hard to resist going too fast. He was shaking and had gotten himself into a situation he had to get out of. Get on down to the platform, then the next one down. Ricky held onto the ladder, his grip so tight, his palms were sweaty. He let one hand go to wipe it on his pants.

No—don't let go—he snapped his hand back to the ladder and forced his foot out to step down another rung. The platform was right under his dangling foot. He could do it—just hop down. Block out the rest of everything. The platform was his "floor" now. *Go—hop down to that. Do it. Get it over with.*

He swung back; his sweaty hands lost their grip— Oomph! Ricky flopped sideways onto the platform and slid off the edge, flailing as he grasped at thin air where he tumbled and plunged. Someone screamed with his voice. Air rushed by his ears and through his hair. This wasn't happening.

I should call on Maggie. What am I waiting for?

The floor rushed up. Men jumped back. One guy lunged to catch him. Missed.

Thud!

* * *

It doesn't hurt.

They stand over me. Stanchfield looks concerned. There's Cheney staring down at me. I don't feel pain. I sit up. My butt is numb. I try to talk. I can't. I look around at the others. They shake their heads.

Stanchfield kneels down. I'm sure he's dead," he says. He sounds far away.

The other guys lower their heads and turn to walk away.

Everyone leaves the area. Stanchfield says he'll call for help, "for what good it'll do."

I feel like drawing a deep breath, but I don't need to. My emotions are nonexistent. I know what happened and I don't care. Maybe I'll figure out why in time. The building must be drafty judging by the rustling of paper and dust around the cavernous lobby. I don't feel a breeze.

I take inventory of my senses. Sight: yes. Hearing: yes. Smell: no. I should be able to smell the painted walls, but don't. Touch: I put my palms onto the floor's wood planks: No. I don't feel the floor. My hands are translucent. As are my legs and torso. I stand and decide to go touch the wall of a room that protrudes into the wide hallway, the room destined for the principal. I haven't been sinking into the floor but then, apparently there's nothing of me for gravity's pull. That explains my hands and butt not feeling the floor. I go to the protruding wall: my hand passes through it, so I press all of me against it and step through the wall. The room's empty except for some small clutter of construction materials.

I go back into the hallway as a car pulls up somewhere outside. Somebody opens the front doors and people enter the building. I look at my hands, feet, waist. I'm mostly translucent, barely visible. Men's voices come from where I fell. I watch the people. That's my body lying there where I fell.

Stanchfield is talking to several people who are strapping it onto a stretcher.

"Is he dead?" Stanchfield says.

"He's dead," says one of the men. "That's an awful fall from that high onto a floor like this."

"Does he have kin?" asks Stanchfield. "Is he engaged or promised?"

My emotions rush back, slamming into me.

Maggie!

I had my chance to approach her. I blew it.

The men carry the stretcher out the front door and their conversation fades.

Maggie!

March 9, 1918

Move-in

The beautiful new, almost imposing building stood before her. Maggie lugged her box of things, balancing it on her hip as she shuffled up the concrete steps to the double doors that were propped open. Inside the cavernous entryway, the hallways greeted her with echoing noises bouncing around the halls from the weekend shift construction workers and the distant clomp-clomp of footsteps reverberating from a teacher moving in.

Maggie hesitated. Right in front of her was the site of the tragedy. She looked up at the ceiling. "I can't help saying it: I can't believe it," she muttered. The ceiling work was complete now, and the whole area looked neat. She repositioned the box on her hip and proceeded on, ascending the staircase. After lugging the box up to the landing, she stopped and caught her breath.

"Oh, dear Ricky, you poor fellow," she said. "Such a terrible thing. I'm so sorry. What a handsome fellow you were, and you must have had a handsome personality to match. I wish we'd gotten to know each other more. If only I knew you were all right."

A breeze wafted in through the open doors below, causing a far-off classroom door to slam. Maggie tapped her hand to her chest and smiled. A moment later, somebody emerged from a hallway below and called up to her. "All right if I close these doors?"

"Yes! Thank you!" she replied.

She carried the box up the last flight and walked along the locker-lined hallway to her classroom on the left. Her room greeted her with shiny wood floors and the smell of fresh wall paint. School staff had kindly arranged the desks in neat rows. Her big wooden desk sat at the front with a green chalkboard on the north wall behind it. The board was fresh and new, devoid of any chalk use. A fresh box of chalk sat at one end of the board tray next to a couple of new erasers. Someone had thought to leave portraits of Washington and Lincoln leaning against the wall beneath the board for her to use at her discretion. She set her box of things down on the desk and pulled out *Classics for the Kansas Schools – Eighth Grade* and set it on her desk, sighed, and looked around the room. Everything was so modern. She turned back to the chalkboard and took out a new piece of chalk. One of the little pleasures of being a teacher: On the middle of the board, she wrote, "Miss Stilwell, 8th Grade English." She then went back to her desk to the box of things and put the items away into a drawer. After that, Maggie decided to tour the school. She went out across the wide hallway, walked down the side hall, and peeked into the first room on the left. A teacher was arranging his desk.

"Well, hello, Miss Stilwell," he said, looking up.

"Mr. Fielding? You'll be teaching here now?"

"Apparently I'm shifting from geometry back to eighth grade math. Seems I'm needed more here than at the high school."

"It'll be nice to have you here," she said. "Was that your door that closed suddenly?"

"I nearly jumped ten feet." He pointed to a chalk streak across the board. "See that?"

"They just closed the front doors so you're safe now," she said.

He smiled and nodded. "Say," he said lowering his voice, "I won't presume to intrude, but I hope you're not taking poor Mr. Austin's tragedy too hard. I've been dealing with it the best I can."

"I appreciate your candor," she said. "It is so hard to believe he's gone, but I'm so busy now, so I'm coping."

"Getting ready for Monday?" he asked.

She nodded. "My students are excited."

"As are the grade school kids housed in the library basement," he said.

"It'll be great to see their eager faces when they arrive, won't it?" Maggie smiled and continued along the hallway past another classroom on the left. It didn't look moved in yet; it was the science classroom with lab tables and fixtures for water and propane. Beyond that room were the restrooms and the end of the hall. She stepped into the girls' restroom and was impressed with the modern fixtures and plumbing.

The hallways formed a large U-shape that enclosed the gym. People were setting up the library along the south hall of the "U" so she didn't go there.

She returned to her room and looked around more.

Principal Nibert tapped on the door jamb's woodwork and leaned in. "Hello, Miss Stilwell," he said. "We received a telegram from Topeka that State Superintendent Ross has accepted our invitation to be here for the school dedication on the 25th."

"Wonderful," she said. "I assume the school will be ready, since we're already allowed to move in."

"Mr. Mueller assured me it will."

"I am ready," said Maggie.

Nibert looked around at her neatly-arranged room. "I see that. Thank you." He returned to the hallway and left.

A few minutes later, satisfied she didn't really need to do anything else, she decided to head home.

* * *

She walked her former route home as when she taught at Eastside School a couple of years before, Third Street to Main Street, then to the right toward her rooming home. When she reached North Main Street, she slowed down as she went by Ricky's rooming house. A man walked to the front door. It looked for a moment as if the man were Ricky, but she dismissed that. The man soon entered the home and was no longer there. Maggie trudged on past and reached the Oxford.

March 9, 1918

Ricky

The building is empty and darker now, but it was good to see Maggie today. I would have laughed if I could when the door blew shut, but she still seems down and I wish I could help lighten her mood somehow and also let her know how I feel about her. I had my chance and I guess I learned my lesson about taking care of business when you can, but well… She wanted to know if I was all right: if a chance draft can bring her a brief smile of joy and ease her mind, then that's good a thing. When she told Mr. Fielding about her busy schedule, she said she is coping. For that, I am glad.

I'm at the top of the stairs now, above the front entrance. Now that it's late and the school is mostly dark, except for small lights in open doorways and ambient light from street lamps spilling in through windows, I can move about the building freely. Since I am translucent, I risk being seen during the day. I have heard that some people stay in school for a long time, but I never thought I would be staying for who knows how long. I have to admit, aside from the sadness of why I'm here, there are little pleasures like walking through walls and exploring around, although I can only roam around the hallways and rooms when the school is empty even at night. I slipped up last week when I thought no one was here and I had to dash by Mr. Martin to dive through a wall.

He muttered something like, "Be gone, whatever you are. All I need is to be seeing things. They'll put me away for sure."

I like to think things through while pacing along the second-floor main hallway and around the other halls. I must have walked these halls hundreds of times already. I wonder if I will endlessly roam, moping about Maggie. I'm not sure how long I'll be able to tolerate the sorrow we both must be experiencing. She will heal eventually; at least I hope she will. She might wonder what I thought of her and what might have been.

Perhaps I flatter myself. Maybe I was just a passing interest, a curiosity. If true, so be it. She's a special person. I wish I'd at least gotten to know her better. Although I did feel a connection with her when I fell from the scaffolding. I'll mull these things over for a long, long time.

I head along the upper main hall toward the south wing that leads off to the left. The library is down that way. There are a lot of windows in there. I go there, slip in and notice the absence of moonbeams streaming in. I look out the window toward the southwestern horizon and get a glimpse of a thin crescent, so there'll be a full moon in about a week and a half. Something I can look forward to. Anyway, I can lean out windows and not risk being seen on dark nights like this, so I have plenty to occupy me in addition to exploring the classrooms. Each teacher has a different approach to room arrangement.

But tonight, I want to try something new. I've been wishing I could interact with solid objects; it would help me feel more "normal."

The library door is locked, but I want to find a door that's a bit ajar so I can try pushing it. I step through the wall back to the hallway and start along, skipping the boys' restroom—its door-closer mechanism too tight, so

I go down to the first floor to walk along the main hallway. The gym doors are too heavy to try. The principal's office is locked. The teacher's lounge is locked.

Ah! The gym stage has curtains. I head in, go up onto the stage and stand by one side of an opened curtain, but it's dark here and even I need some light for detailed work. I'll wait until dawn and hide behind the curtain to try it.

I spend the rest of the night wandering around, thinking about Maggie. Even in my state of being, my emotion is strong, like when it rushed back into me after my fall. Am I an entity only of emotion? I can't be. I don't want to be. But I know Maggie is strong—I need to give her credit for being able to get over it.

Enough pondering this for now. I'll explore until there's a little light, then go back to the stage.

* * *

Pre-dawn fades in outside. The sun won't be up for a while. An early-riser enters the building. I go to the stage curtain and place the back of my hand against the fabric—my hand just passes through it. Pulling my hand back, I concentrate. If I had teeth, I'd be gritting them now with my face straining as I press my hand against the curtain. Movement! The curtain barely twitched with an ever-so-slight flutter, but it did move against my hand. If this works then I can do it, but I can't strain like that every time just to interact with a solid. Think…what all did I do to achieve success? Was there one thing? Think.

I try it again, more concentration this time. If I had a voice, I'd be groaning. Movement. But no more than the first try.

Why didn't that move it more?

46

I don't have to breathe, but I feel like taking in a deep sigh, and I fling the back of my translucent hand against the curtain.

More movement this time. The curtain flickers.

What was it? My minor rage? Breathing?

Another try.

I take a deep breath and hold it. I try again and push the curtain.

The curtain waves a bit. I can do it!

My goal for some semblance of normalcy is closer, not yet achieved.

I'll keep trying.

March 25, 1918

Maggie

Maggie and Rose entered the gymnasium where modern lighting provided a bright gathering place for the people assembled at the dedication program. Rose led Maggie to one of the refreshments tables.

"I thought we should get something before you have to go up to your room for the public tour."

"Thank you. I do want to listen to the State Superintendent's address before I leave the gym."

They found seats. After a few minutes, local Board of Education President Dr. Bower went to the podium on the stage at the end of the gym. The audience quieted as he introduced soloist Maurine Smith who entertained the gathered attendees with two songs, followed by resounding applause. Dr. Bower then introduced a tall, trim young-looking State Superintendent W. D. Ross, who thanked the crowd for attending and complimented the people of Eureka for building "a magnificent and thoroughly up-to-date school building." He started his address by insisting more attention be given to the physical well-being of the students in light of twenty-nine percent of Selective Service-registered men being rejected because of physical deficiencies.

When his address wrapped up, Maggie leaned over to Rose. "I'm afraid I need to get up to my classroom," she said.

"I'll go with you," offered Rose.

"Of course, but don't be surprised if there's more than you planned on."

Rose smiled. "I'll help in any way. Let's go."

They stood and gave apologetic looks to others as they made their way to the gym's exit. Everything was well lit out in the main hall that led to the front staircase.

Maggie pointed to the protruding office near the staircase. "That's the principal's office," she said, which distracted her attention from the accident location ahead. She took a deep breath as they headed toward the stairs and veered around that spot.

"It was there, wasn't it?" said Rose, nodding ahead.

"Yes," answered Maggie in a quiet tone.

"I'm sorry," said Rose.

"No, Rose, I know you're sad, too. I know I seem like it's just me who is mourning."

"Really, Maggie, I understand."

"Well then," Maggie said, lightening her tone, "let me show you my classroom."

They skipped up the stairs and reached the second floor. Down the lighted hallway they went, along the lockers toward Maggie's classroom. All the rooms were well lit and teachers waited near their doors for visitors. George Fielding stood in his doorway and smiled as the two women approached Maggie's room which was also well lit. When they reached it, Maggie invited Rose to go in first. As soon as she entered, a flash with a "tck" sound sent the room into darkness and she rushed back out.

A second later, both of them shrieked to a loud crash in the dim room.

"Wait here, Rose," said Maggie. Ambient light from the hall was enough to go in and look around the room. The portrait of Washington lay ruined on the floor.

Rose stepped in after her. "I barely missed getting hit by that!"

Maggie put her arm on Rose's shoulder and led her back out into the hall. "The light burned out," she said. "What bad timing. I'm really glad you didn't get hit—are you all right?"

"Just a little shaken," said Rose, taking a deep breath. "I'm fine now."

"I'll find Mr. Martin and see if he can replace the bulb and help me clean that up."

George Fielding walked over to them. "Are you both all right?" he asked.

"Bulb burned out," said Maggie. "Hopefully, Mr. Martin is handy."

"I'll go find him," offered George.

"Well—" started Maggie.

"It's fine," he said. "I've got my room ready. You stay and do what you need while I go fetch him."

"I'll stand by your door," Rose said to him.

"That's all right, thanks," he said, "I'll write a note on the board."

Maggie thanked George and he left.

Maggie and Rose peered into Maggie's dim classroom.

"I want to take a good look around," Maggie said. "I think it's ready, but there may be some last-minute things."

"Would you like some help?" said Rose.

"You're welcome to just keep me company and I'll make sure the Lincoln portrait looks secure!"

They went to Maggie's desk and Maggie nudged a few items into alignment on the desktop. She moved the wax apple to the corner.

"Do kids still bring apples?" Rose asked, picking it up.

"They do. One of my students gave me this for our move from the temporary high school space," said

Maggie. "I think she meant it to symbolize that this room is permanent unlike the high school attic and an actual apple."

Footsteps in the hallway.

Mr. Martin entered the room carrying a tall step ladder. "Bulb out?" he asked.

"Thank you for being so handy," said Maggie.

"I'm ready tonight in case of this very kind of thing and I'm also here so I can show off the new boiler, completely modern," he said while positioning the ladder. He climbed it and reached up to the bulb. "I'm surprised a new bulb burned out so quickly." He removed the cover to expose the wiring.

"Something there?' asked Maggie.

"Just checking for a short," he said aiming his bulky flashlight into the recessed area. "Hm, well, I don't think there was a short, but I'll have our electrician look at it." He replaced the bulb, lighting up the room. "Now then," he said as he climbed down the ladder. "I'll take care of that picture."

"It was the strangest thing," said Rose.

He deposited debris into his rolling cart's bag, set the picture and frame aside and then placed the ladder next to the wall, climbing up to look at the area. "Who mounted these pictures?" he asked.

"One of the workmen put these up for me on his break," said Maggie.

"I'll check the Lincoln one in a moment. This one wasn't secure. I'm not surprised it gave way." He replaced the hook, hung the portrait, and said, "There. It'll need new glass, but it won't fall again." He went to check the Lincoln portrait. "Looks fine," he said.

Maggie sighed.

"People are arriving," Mr. Martin said, "so I'll get out of your way and go back down to the boiler room." He took the ladder and left.

"I'd like to look around, too," said Rose.

"Yes. Be sure to see the library and go down to Mr. Martin's boiler room and also see some of the first-floor rooms."

* * *

Rose joined a line of people rounding the second-floor classrooms. She broke from the line at the library. The room looked about the size of one and a half classrooms with the north and east walls lined with bookcases and tables arranged in the center area. A long bulletin board that ran lengthwise above the bookcases had pictures of children reading and other encouraging display materials.

Annie approached Rose.

"Hello, Rose," she said. "Welcome to the school library." She led Rose to the counter near the west wall. "This counter is where students can request information and check books out."

As Rose was looking at a sample library card, a giggling girl and boy with several others and a woman at a chalkboard on wheels distracted her.

"One of our programs for tonight," said Annie.

She and Rose walked over to them.

The board had dozens of names written by the young students.

"This is nice," said Rose.

"We played a name game," the woman said, smiling.

The giggling girl tapped the woman's arm.

"Yes, Mary?" the woman asked. "What is it?"

"He didn't spell my name right," Mary whispered, "because he doesn't write his letters very well."

"I do, too," the boy said. "My hand didn't go the way I wanted it."

"It's all right, Mary," the woman said. "He starts school in a few months."

52

The woman smiled at Rose. "She takes her big sister role seriously."

Rose acknowledged the woman, thanked Annie, and went to the hallway to follow the group down to the first floor and then toward the gymnasium.

Principal Nibert greeted them at one of the entrances.

"If you'll follow me in, ladies and gentlemen, I'll show you how modern our new gymnasium is." He gathered everyone to the middle of the gym and gestured around. "Notice the double deck observation galleries, each accessed through entrances from the first and second floors. The galleries have a total seating capacity of two hundred fifty." He pointed up. "The climbing ropes are well secured to the ceiling, and the basketball goals are regulation height."

Principal Nibert started toward the stage. "We'll all enjoy performances on this fine stage for many years to come." People went to it, some sliding their fingertips across the stage floor.

After some chatter among the visitors about watching their kids up there one day, the principal brought Mr. Martin over.

"Now, ladies and gentlemen, Mr. Martin will show you the modern boiler and fuel room."

Rose and the others followed Mr. Martin down the southeast stairs to the basement level and entered a corridor with a couple of doors on the left. They walked past a wider hall that went off to the right and continued on to a room where Mr. Martin stood next to an open door.

When it was Rose's section's turn to look in, Mr. Martin gestured into the room to a cylinder-shaped boiler with a smooth, rounded upper end and a pressure gauge on top. The bottom rested on a somewhat small box-shaped base surrounded by plumbing.

"This boiler will keep your children warm in winter," said Mr. Martin. "The furnace is quite secure. Your children will be protected from fire as this boiler room is built without any openings leading to the main building. A fire wouldn't be transmitted to the classrooms. It's a very efficient, safe system."

Several people lingered as Mr. Martin concluded his presentation. Rose went with the group up to the first floor, to the domestic science room, the woman with her two children still behind her.

Rose kneeled down to the girl. "You and your brother did a good job at the name game," she said.

The girl smiled. "Danny spelled my name 'M S R A', but he's just a little boy," she said.

"Why yes," said Rose. "He'll get better at it." Rose stood as the line started to move into the room where they viewed kitchen and other appliances, some of them more modern than Rose's own. After viewing the model dining room, Rose went back up to Maggie's room. Maggie had a group of people around her as she answered questions.

Early May 1918

Delinquents

One Friday evening toward the end of the semester, the school building looked imposing in the twilight.

"We go in, fix it, and get out, see?" Jackie said, getting on his hands and knees below the window.

"You sure you opened it a little? It doesn't look like it," Andy said.

"Hurry up and get on my back," Jackie said. "I snuck into the room and cracked the window open before I left."

Andy climbed onto Jackie's back and pulled himself up to the window sill. He reached into the gap and grunted as he shoved the window up. "Phew! Should we do this?" he said.

"Criminy, you want us to get into high school next year or you want to stay in eighth grade?"

"All right." Andy hoisted himself through the window and reached out to pull Jackie up.

Jackie tumbled in, caught his breath, and they straightened the desk they had knocked aside, and tiptoed through the classroom.

"Is this third grade?" Andy said.

"Yeah, it's third grade. So what?"

"We don't want to end up back here, either," Andy said.

"We will if you don't shut up," Jackie said. He led the way toward the door.

A distant thump boomed.

"What was that?" whispered Andy, crouching now.

"Forget about it," Jackie said. "Old Martin's done in these rooms. Look how clean the board is."

As they stepped into the hallway, Andy gazed to the shadowy end. "I don't like it here at night and I think my grades are good enough to pass anyway," he whispered.

"Well, mine aren't," Jackie said. "Yours might not be, either." He stepped across the hall and opened the gym door and looked in. A small light at one end scarcely cut through the gloom.

"What are we doing here?" whispered Andy.

"Look how swell this looks at night. Want to do some one-on-one if I can find a ball?" He pointed to the far basketball goal.

"No," Andy said.

"Come on, you big baby."

Jackie led Andy out across the gym floor. Distant knocking sounds faded and an outside door closed.

"Martin's left," Jackie said. "Let's play."

"There's no ball."

Jackie trotted to the far goal and ran like he was making a lay-up, pretended to toss a ball to Andy. He ran out to the free throw line. "Run toward me for a hand off."

Andy just slumped. "I don't want to."

"Aww." Jackie ran to the goal and almost tripped over something. "Look! A ball!"

He scooped it up and dribbled over to Andy. "Think fast!" He tossed the ball to Andy's face, got it back, then dribbled out to half court. "Watch this." He lobbed the ball to the goal and hit the rim, the ball bounced back.

"Can we get this over with?" pleaded Andy.

"All right. Let's go." They went toward the exit to the main hallway and Jackie flipped the ball over his shoulder into the gloom where it bounced behind them, the bounces fading away, then gone.

They went out the gym exit to the main hallway and went to the front stairway.

"Hey," Jackie said, pointing to the accident area. "That's where that guy fell when they were building this place."

"I heard about it," Andy said. "I heard Miss Stilwell liked him."

"But did he like her?" Jackie said. "I doubt it. Come on."

After reaching the stairs, they crept up to the landing.

"Wait here," Jackie said.

"You're not leaving me alone here," Andy said.

"No, stupid, I need to double check the coast is clear."

Jackie crawled up the last half flight and peeked at the second-floor main hallway. He gave Andy a thumbs-up and waved him up. "Definitely nobody here," he said when Andy climbed up.

They walked down the hall toward Maggie's classroom, Jackie dragging his fingers along the lockers. When they reached Maggie's classroom door, Jackie tried to open it.

"Locked…as I figured." He took a hairpin from his pocket. "I didn't think my mother would miss this tonight." He picked the lock, opened the door, and went into the room, some light coming from outside street lamps casting a rectangle onto Maggie's desk. Andy started to follow Jackie in.

"No," Jackie said. "Keep watch. I'll take care of everything." He picked the desk drawer lock. "Here it is." He grabbed the gradebook and a pen and took them to a window, opened the shade, and spread the gradebook across the window sill in the direct light of a street lamp.

"Let's see," he said taking the pen. "Fourth quarter final grades." He started writing.

"Andy, my 'F' is now a 'B' and I'm changing some of my weekly grades to match the final grade. Hey, Andy, I'm smart. I went from an 'F' to a 'B'. Could have been to an 'A', but I'm not greedy. A 'B' and I'll pass English."

Andy laughed. "What about mine? How do they look"

Jackie looked through the book for a while. "Hm, yours could be better." He closed the gradebook and took it back to the desk. "It'd take me an hour. We got to get going."

"But you said—"

"I can't do it. You should have shown me your grade cards before tonight so I could be ready.

"You didn't tell me to. If you hadn't found that basketball, we'd have had more time, darn you."

Jackie tossed the gradebook into the desk drawer and left it to run to the door. "Not my fault you didn't think of the cards. Now, if you want to get in trouble, stay here. I'm leaving."

Jackie didn't lock the drawer or Maggie's door, so after he left, Andy thought about going to get the gradebook out, but he didn't want to go into the room by himself.

He had never been in a dark, quiet classroom, full of empty chairs and desks.

The gradebook tipped itself to the top of the desk. It slid across the desk and fell to the floor and moved across the floor.

"J-J-Jackie!"

Jackie responded, his voice far away.

Andy ran down the hall, leaving the classroom door open and rushed to the front stairs. Down he ran to the landing. Maggie's door slammed shut as he ran, echoing throughout, bouncing from hall to hall. He nearly tripped hurrying down to the front doors. Locked. He ran to the third-grade classroom, to the window. Jackie had closed it on his way out so Andy had to heave it open in a panic and pull himself through. He dropped to the ground and ran home.

Early May 1918

Maggie

The following Monday around midday, an anxious Maggie sat in Principal Nibert's office while Mr. Nibert leaned back and looked through a folder. A knock at the door. Mr. Martin entered.

Mr. Nibert pointed to a chair. "Have a seat."

Mr. Martin nodded a greeting to Maggie and sat.

"What's the trouble, Mr. Nibert?" he said. "They said it was urgent."

Mr. Nibert nodded. "Do you remember approximate times of your duties this past Friday evening and on Saturday?"

"I reckon I do," answered Mr. Martin. "I finished my usual rounds Friday night and ended by sweeping the south hall on the second floor."

"Were you anywhere near Miss Stilwell's classroom?"

"As usual, I took care of her room during my classroom rounds and finished hers and Mr. Fielding's around nine-thirty. What's wrong? I didn't have much to do on Saturday this time."

Maggie took a deep breath. "My gradebook is missing."

"Oh my word," said Mr. Martin. "I have no idea about that."

"Nobody's accusing you," said Mr. Nibert. "We're just looking for clues."

"Come to think of it," Mr. Martin offered. "Something strange on Saturday. A window in Miss Hendricks's classroom was left open. She's always good at leaving her room in good order, so I figured something came up. I assume nothing's wrong in there?"

"No, all is fine there," said Mr. Nibert. "But we're puzzled about the gradebook. You didn't notice anything unusual in Miss Stilwell's classroom?"

"One of the window shades was pulled up a little."

"We're just looking at everything."

"May I ask," said Mr. Martin." He looked at Maggie. "How did you discover it was missing?"

"I need to turn in final grades and was set to start on that early this morning, but my gradebook wasn't in my drawer where I'd left it."

"Was the drawer closed and locked when you got in? asked Mr. Nibert.

"Locked just like I left it when I went home," she said.

"And your room?" asked Mr. Nibert.

"Locked."

"Keep looking as thoroughly as possible," said Mr. Nibert. "We'll help."

"I'll do everything I can," Mr. Martin said.

Maggie and Mr. Martin got up and left the office. In the hallway, Maggie ignored her usual habit of veering around the accident scene and carried her lunch bucket into the gym. Some of the eight-graders were sitting at a table near the stage. She went past the table toward the teachers' table.

"Miss Stilwell?" said Carolyn. "Would you like to sit at our table?" She gestured to the empty seat.

The other students nodded and she joined them at the end of the table. As soon as she settled in, one of her students got up to leave.

* * *

An hour later, when the student was on his way to two o'clock study hall, he was having second thoughts about their sneaking into the school Friday night. Then he realized he'd misplaced his math book that he wanted to study for a test Mr. Fielding was letting him retake the next day. He first went by his morning classes to see if he'd left it in one of those. Not finding it, he went to his locker. The book was nowhere within the stacks of things in there. He had English class coming up in an hour so he wouldn't have left it in Miss Stilwell's class, but he wanted to check everywhere, even in places he felt it couldn't be.

Miss Stilwell was sitting at her desk when he entered her classroom.

"Miss Stilwell?" he said.

She looked up. "Yes, come in, Andrew."

He went to his usual desk. "I can't find my math book and wanted to see if it's here.

He looked around, but didn't notice it anywhere.

Disappointed, he sighed.

"Not finding it?" she said.

"No."

"I'm sorry. I know how you feel," she said. "I've misplaced my gradebook and it's nowhere to be found and I need it. It was right here in my drawer."

"Well," started Andy. But he caught himself.

"Well what?"

"Oh nothing." He sat at his desk and regarded her. She was in great distress. He could still borrow a math book and Mr. Fielding might even let him study from the teacher's edition now that the quarter was ending. It was time to own up to it. So he summoned his nerves.

"Miss Stilwell? I have to tell you something."

She looked up, expectantly.

"I'm sorry," Andy said, nearly crying. "Jackie and I snuck in here Friday night."

"Yes?"

We—he—got your gradebook out to change our grades."

Her expression relaxed. "I'll ask later how you got in here, but I'd like my gradebook back now, please."

"I don't have it. Neither does Jackie. He put it back in your drawer and we left."

Her expression soured. "Then you don't have any idea where it is?"

"No, honest. I'm sorry, we shouldn't have come in. I won't ever do it again!"

She stood. "We'll deal with all that later. You and Jackie could get kicked out of school or at minimum fail eighth grade, which would make your little scheme backfire."

Andy started crying and stood. As he started to turn toward the door, through bleary eyes, something in the bookcase caught his attention. He wiped his eyes and spotted a blue book sitting in plain sight on a shelf.

"Miss Stilwell! There it is!" He skipped over to the bookcase and lifted his math book up.

The gradebook sat there, it had been under the math book.

Maggie jumped for joy and retrieved the gradebook.

"I'll write you a pass to miss the first of study hall if you stay to go over your grades."

"Um. Well."

"I wanted to talk to you about it, anyway."

"All right." He sat down and she sat at the desk next to him and opened the gradebook to his record.

"Now, let's see," she said, scanning across. "Hm. Your grades are better than I remember." She frowned at him. "Now Andy, did you or Jackie in fact change your grades?"

"No, Miss Stilwell, not mine. Jackie changed his but wouldn't do mine."

She looked at the record again. "Now that I look closely, that's my handwriting. But Jackie certainly did change his grades using an old trick, but he a did a convincing job. I might not have caught it."

"I didn't watch him."

"Now your grades...the March test shows a 'B' in my gradebook. I remembered you maybe getting a 'C' on it, but maybe I forgot, because that's my handwriting, no doubt about it as are my marks all across your record. Your grades are good enough to pass this course, so you didn't need to be dishonest."

"I didn't think my grades were bad," he said.

"Now there's the matter of you sneaking in that we need to deal with."

"It's my only time ever. I won't do it again. Please don't report me?"

"Well. I appreciate your honesty even when you were upset about losing your own book. It must have been hard to tell me."

"It wasn't hard. I had to tell you."

"I think we can keep this between us, but it's obvious now that Jackie's grades were changed by someone besides me and I might not have noticed that and passed him."

"Is he going to get in trouble?"

"He'll fail and have to repeat Eighth Grade English before he graduates junior high. It'll be a lesson that cheating doesn't pay."

"He won't like being held back."

"Maybe we should send him back to third grade," she said, smiling.

Andy let a chuckle slip out.

Now Maggie had to figure out the best way to help Jackie.

Maggie

A couple of weeks later, Maggie decided she needed an outfit for the coming warmer weather and Frank H. Brooks was having a sale. Best to take advantage of that, what with everything getting more expensive these days. She headed down the porch steps of the Oxford and strolled along Main Street. When she passed Ricky's rooming house, she felt a dull ache in her stomach, but thoughts of those mornings when he was there on the porch watching her walk by made her smile. She stopped and pretended to adjust her hat as she gazed up to the porch chair where he usually was. She thought she caught a glimpse of him in his chair with coffee, flashing a smile so she wiggled her fingers to pretend to wave at the imaginary man as if he were sitting there. The imaginary Ricky winked and she went on.

There was Rose up ahead walking toward her.

When they met, Rose said, "It's nice to see you smile."

"I was thinking about when I used to walk by here," said Maggie. "Every morning, he sat there with his coffee and last time, I waved like this." She held up her hand and wiggled her fingers.

"Well, weren't you a flirt?" said Rose.

"I always wave like that," said Maggie.

"Of course you do. And I've noticed that you still walk by there often."

"It helps to remember those little things," said Maggie. "I think I'm dealing with the tragedy better as time goes by, but I don't know. I wish I knew why Ricky was doing something dangerous when he was new. Sometimes I get angry. I don't feel all together sometimes."

"You hide it well."

"But I feel it inside. It helps that I've been so busy with the school year ending."

"I'm glad of that. Now…are you ready for the sale?"

Maggie shrugged. "I think so. I'm not an avid shopper like some. I don't much care, but I do need something for hot weather."

"Then I'll help you," said Rose.

"Wonderful. I need to stop by the bank first."

"All right. See you at Brooks."

Rose went on her way and Maggie continued on toward the corner of Third and Main. The diagonal side of the ornate building with the large embedded stone letters "BANK" at the top dominated that side of the intersection, rivaled by the Greenwood Hotel which dominated the corner across from there.

She reached Citizens National Bank, entered the lobby, and approached the paneled wooden counter under the "Savings Department" sign.

A teller greeted her from behind the cage bars. "Hello, Miss Stilwell," he said.

She acknowledged him and went to the counter. "Hello," she said. "I'd like to withdraw nine dollars and with two of the dollars, I'd like to buy eight twenty-five-cent War thrift stamps."

"Oh, yes," the teller said, getting into a drawer. "Do you have a card started?"

"No, this is my first purchase."

He unfolded a card on the table. "These sixteen squares are where you can affix the thrift stamps. I'll attach your first eight now if you'd like." He set the card's envelope next to it. "Please fill in your name and address here. And congratulations on helping the war effort. Every stamp sold shortens the duration. The bottom explains what the value will be in 1923."

"Thank you," she said, looking at the card. It gave her a good feeling. She placed the card and envelope into her bag and left. Out on the sidewalk, she started down toward the Frank H. Brooks store about a block and a half away.

When she entered the store, the smell of new clothes greeted her as always. After browsing a while, she ran into Rose.

"Oh!" said Rose, a dress draped across her arm. "I wanted to show you—"

"Is that intended for me?" Maggie asked.

Rose held the dress up. "Will you try it on? I know the material's a bit revealing, but it's lightweight and comfortable, especially during summer."

"I know I tend to be modest. As a teacher, I try to present a proper appearance."

"This isn't for school. It's a summer outfit for when you're not in school."

Maggie ran her fingers along the flowing material. "And what if some of my students happen to be out and see me in this? And I do have a couple of summer students."

Rose shrugged, handed the dress to her. "Don't wear it on those days," she said, leading her to the dressing room. "Try it on."

After much consideration, Maggie bought the dress and two other garments and she left the store with Rose. They walked up the sidewalk.

"The sun feels nice today," said Rose, "but it won't be long before it's overbearing. Good thing you got those outfits."

Having some cash left after her purchase, Maggie led Rose to Mac's Newsstand store on Second and Main Streets where a teenaged boy held a piece of candy out along with his other hand, palm up, to a younger boy who reached into his pocket. Maggie and Rose went into Mac's and browsed a bit while Mac arranged items on the counter.

He reached under the counter. "We got a couple of new books in, Maggie. I saved one back for you."

"Thank you, Mac," said Maggie. "I'll have some time to read now with the school year over."

He set an Edgar Rice Burroughs book onto the counter.

Maggie picked the book up and flipped through some pages. "Just the thing to distract from reality for a while," she said.

"I thought so, too," he said. "How are you getting along?"

"I'm well, thank you," she said as she paid for the book.

"Are you going to be involved with Commencement?" Rose asked her.

"We have it this Friday." Maggie said.

Mac put Maggie's book into a bag. "Are they holding the ceremony up at the Princess Theatre again?" he asked.

"Yes," she said, "Although one of my students failed English and won't receive his diploma then."

Mac shook his head. "That's too bad."

"He's being given a chance to pass with summer study," she said.

"I'm glad to know that," he said.

She thanked him, took her bag, and went to the door with Rose.

"Keep looking up, Maggie," Mac said while she and Rose headed out to the sidewalk.

"I'll head on now," said Rose. "You probably want to get home. Looks like rain." She kissed Maggie's cheek and went on her way.

Maggie hurried down the sidewalk toward the Oxford, and it started sprinkling when she reached Third Street. She picked up the pace, skipping along under the storefront awnings. She wanted to get home so she could spend the next couple of hours reading and managed to stay dry enough as the rain hit.

When she got home, up to her room, she freshened up a little and put her new garments away. After running around all day, she splashed water from the basin onto her face then brushed out her hair and pinned it back. As she went to grab her new book to take down to the living room to read until dinner, a knock at her door interrupted her.

"Maggie? Are you in?"

She opened the door for Lydia Thrall, the owner of the rooming house.

"Mr. and Mrs. Austin are here to see you," said Mrs. Thrall. "They're waiting in the living room. They are welcome to stay for dinner if you'd like to invite them."

"Thank you, Mrs. Thrall. I shall be down shortly."

Mrs. Thrall nodded and left. Maggie went back to her dresser mirror, adjusted her hair and straightened her jacket lapels while wondering who her guests were. She went out to the long hallway and downstairs to the well-adorned living room where a man and woman in about their early thirties sat on the Queen Anne sofa next to the bay windows. They smiled as Maggie stepped off the stairs and approached them.

They stood and the man said, "Hello, Miss Stilwell, I am Clyde Austin, Ricky's cousin and this is my wife, Marie. We're here from El Dorado."

"Glad to meet you," said Maggie, offering her hand. "Please make yourself at home." She sat in the chair that faced them. "This is a pleasant surprise," she said when they settled back onto the sofa.

"We're sorry to call unannounced," said Marie.

"That's quite all right," said Maggie. "I'm glad to meet Ricky's relatives."

"Ricky was an only child and I'm his only surviving relative," said Clyde. "His parents, my aunt and uncle, died five years ago. Ricky was heartbroken, but resilient and worked to better himself after he finished high school. He wanted to be an architect someday and was thrilled to get the job with Mueller Construction, and wrote that it would be a start for him and good training in advance of study. Then we didn't hear from him and didn't know why. We learned of his accident later."

"It was quite a shock," said Marie.

"We're all sad about it at the school," said Maggie, suppressing a sniffle. "I'm happy to know this about Ricky, but how or why did you seek me out?"

"He wrote to us about you," said Clyde.

"Oh, dear," said Maggie. "I had no idea. I had already been walking by his rooming house most every day before he arrived in Eureka and after a while, I ran into him at the post office. After that on my walks by his home, I started noticing his glances, and his seeming shyness began to endear him to me. And we went to a play with friends a couple of days before the accident. We were finally getting to know each other and I expected we would have a chance at courting."

"Have you heard the expression, 'love at first sight'?" asked Marie.

Maggie brought a handkerchief to her eyes.

"I didn't mean to—" said Marie.

"Show her the card holder," said Clyde.

"Of course." Marie retrieved it from her purse and handed it to Maggie. Engraved on the face of the card holder was

Richard Austin

Architect

Presented September 14, 1916

Marie leaned toward Maggie. "After he met you, Ricky wrote that he wanted you to have this if anything ever happened to him," she said. "We had had it made for his twenty-fourth birthday a couple of years ago."

Maggie clasped her hands around it and held it to her chest. "But should it remain with his family?"

"No, he wanted you to have it," said Clyde.

"I'd love to have it. Are there other young ladies who caught his interest?"

"Perhaps," said Clyde, "but only causally. He never talked about anyone else like he did about you. On our last visit, he imagined what you might be like and said he wasn't sure he'd be worthy of you."

Maggie broke down.

Marie came over and kneeled next to her chair and took her hand.

"I'm sorry, Maggie," said Clyde leaning on his palms. "I should let Marie do the talking."

Maggie shook her head. "No, Clyde, it's fine. I'll treasure the knowledge as I'll treasure this card holder."

Mrs. Thrall entered the living room.

Maggie smiled at her guests. "I meant to invite to you to stay for dinner. The meals are excellent here."

Maggie held the card holder tightly, as if she'd never let go of it and led the Austins to the dining room.

After dinner, Maggie and her housemates retired to the living room to chat as they often did and Maggie asked the Austins to stay for a while. She enjoyed conversation and her guests added to that as if part of Ricky himself were present. After a while, she noticed her knuckles turning white from gripping the card holder.

Later that night, she sat on her bed, studied the card holder and brought it up to her lips, then held it under the lamp, twisting it back and forth so the light glinted off the engraving with each twist. She eased it open. Nothing inside. Not that she expected there to be.

June 10, 1918

Ricky

After several weeks of quiet around the school, some students and teachers have returned for summer session this morning. I maintain near-invisibility as I sneak around the hallways.

The boy called Jackie—since he got himself in trouble, I believe he might be here today to start the summer make-up session, which would increase the chance that Maggie will be in. Is it right for me to be happy about that when she might not have had to come in? But oh, I sure want to see her.

I'm staying put in a corner at the south end of the second-floor main hallway. Activity is picking up and why is Principal Nibert walking this way with Mr. Mueller?

Stay still, I tell myself.

Nibert looks around, then straight at me. "Let's look at this wall," he says, leaning toward me. "Look at that."

Mueller leans toward me as well.

What are they seeing? Would they notice if I disappeared through the wall? They'd see my silhouette for a split second. Then they'd rub their eyes, and think nothing of it.

"I see it," says Mueller.

Nibert turns to Mueller. "We need to do something before school starts in the fall."

I find that concerning. Do *what* about me?

"We'll take care of it," Mueller says.

"When can you start?"

Mueller rubs his chin. "One of my paint crews will free up next week."

"That's good," Nibert says, "because I don't want parents seeing sloppy work like that. Let's go around to the classrooms."

"Right," Mueller says as he puts his hand on Nibert's shoulder and they continue their conversation down the south hallway.

If I had to breathe for real, I would let out a big sigh. I remain still and watch several students emerge into the main hall from the front stairway. There's Jackie. He walks toward Maggie's class, goes in.

I bide my time until the halls clear.

Mr. Martin comes from the south hall, goes up the main hallway past the lockers and Maggie's classroom then turns down the side hall. The main hallway is clear now. I slide along the walls toward the lockers and stop several times. At one stop, I can look into Mr. Stauffer's Current Events class. He's talking about the War. I pause for a moment and think. The soldiers as they fight in foreign lands for freedom face more danger from a hostile enemy than I from my fear of heights.

I continue sliding along the lockers toward the area across from Maggie's door, which is just ahead. I reach there and stop. I can see through her open door to a corner of her desk and hear her voice for the first time in weeks. It sounds wonderful. If I had a stomach, it would have butterflies. Mr. Martin comes back around the corner. I press against the lockers. He passes by and doesn't notice my silhouette. The patterns in the lockers are camouflaging me. As much as I'd like to slip across the hallway to Maggie's door and spend an hour peeking in at her while she conducts class even with those few summer school students, I decide against it. Besides, I would get so mesmerized, I'd still be there when students exit the classroom.

I am tempted to sneak around and watch other classes in session, but that's risky, too. I don't want to make a mistake and start rumors about the school being haunted. Haunted, indeed. What a concept. No. I'll keep sliding around the walls and pretend to be a blotch on a wall in need of paint. I might be useful so I'll stay put for now.

Then again…something's going on down in the gym.

I make sure the halls are empty and I slip over to the north stairway and slide down the banister to the first floor where I'm close to a gym entrance. I make my way to the door and peek in. There's Jackie trying to balance himself on the side horse near the stage, swinging his legs around.

Coach Marshall is with three students conducting a springboard exercise near the other end of the gym.

"Get off there!" he yells to Jackie.

I go down the hallway outside the gym toward Jackie's end. I want to slip in without being seen, so I need to jump through the wall and move fast.

Here goes. Check up and down the hall. Empty.

Jump! I tumble into a box of basketballs. Several bounce out and roll across the gym, distracting Marshall. Jackie jumps away. I blend into the minor chaos.

Marshall yells at Jackie again. "Get over here!"

Jackie trots over to him. I hear the Coach discussing something with the boy. I sneak along the wall to get closer. Marshall is offering to let him try out for summer gymnastics, but insists he get back to English class first. Jackie agrees but starts to run back toward the other end of the gym toward the side horse.

"Where are you going!" Marshall yells.

"Just one minute to try the side horse!" Jackie yells back.

"It's loose—don't jump on it!"

Jackie runs faster toward it. I dive onto his path and he trips over my barely visible form.

Marshall rushes over and helps him up. "Good thing you tripped over your own two feet! You'd have gotten really hurt on that."

"But…" Jackie searches the floor for what tripped him, doesn't notice me. I don't know if Maggie will discipline him or not. I could teach him a lesson, but perhaps I've interfered enough. The boy needs help.

Jackie looks around. "I'm getting out of here." He runs out to the hall.

June 10, 1918

Jackie

Jackie crept into Maggie's classroom; Carolyn was sitting at a desk in front.

"Where's Miss Stilwell?" he asked her.

She looked toward the door. "I think she's looking for you."

"Am I in trouble?"

"I don't know. She never lets on when she's mad, but I know she doesn't like a sneak."

"I'm not a sneak. I had a late lunch and I wanted to see what they were going to do in the gym."

"They're starting this session of summer gymnastics," she said.

"I know. I got on the side horse."

"You didn't," Carolyn said. "Its handles are loose and Tony slipped off it this morning when he jumped on it. They moved it over by the stage and put a 'keep off' sign on it so nobody would get hurt. They're going to put it away and get it fixed."

"They shouldn't leave it out like that," he said.

She folded her arms. "Who's going to be stupid enough to jump on it with that sign? I hope it's fixed soon and ready for when I start gymnastics next month," she said.

Jackie sneered and sat on the other side of the room from her. He didn't know what Miss Stilwell's plans for him were, so he looked around for a clue. Her copy of one of the readers sat on her desk along with other items. He got up and went to the desk. A sheet of paper with hand-written notes sat on top of some things. As soon as he picked the paper up, he noticed something under it and Carolyn stood and scolded. "What are you doing! Put that down."

He glanced across the desk then set the paper down. "All right, fine." He looked toward the door. "I'm not going to wait forever," he said.

"You need to stay here," she said.

"See you later," he said, going toward the door. He left Carolyn alone shaking her head as he walked out to the hallway and went down the front stairway. He noticed the gym still had some activity and looked in. Miss Stilwell was talking to Coach Marshall. Jackie ducked back and went to the south side hall. Down past the boys and girls locker rooms, he went down the southeast stairway to the basement. Although the basement had a main hallway with doors and a classroom at the north end, the boiler room intrigued him. Old Martin wasn't around and the boiler room door was open. Jackie entered the dim room and ran his hands over the boiler's curved surface, tapping his fingernails on the top, producing a hollow metallic echo. The boiler had a lot of pipes protruding from it leading to joints, branching the pipes in different directions. One had a valve shut-off handle. He took hold of it and tested the tightness. It didn't budge.

A sound like a door opening came from the stairway and the boiler room door slammed shut. He heard steps and hid behind the boiler and crouched low, avoiding detection. Mr. Martin opened the door and looked in, then closed the door. A sound like the door being locked prompted Jackie to check for his trusty hairpin. Mr. Martin's footsteps faded and Jackie felt his way around in the dark to the door, turned the knob and opened the door. So he didn't need to pick the lock, which he didn't understand. He stepped out to the small, dim side-hallway and waited for a while before heading on.

He waited and listened then went up the wide hall to the Art room and tried the door, took the hairpin and picked the lock. The Art room was eerily quiet and as always had interesting smells of oil paint and turpentine with a hint of clay. A couple of easels stood near the chalkboard. He went to the one that held a blank canvas and a tube of red paint on its tray then he looked around for a paint brush. The room was mostly empty except for tables, and a potter's wheel along one wall. The door to the kiln room toward the back was open, so he went there. It was dark, like the boiler room. He stepped in and looked around for a paintbrush. The kiln's door was open and its two shelves were empty. He felt around the top of it, no paintbrush there. Nor did the shelves on the wall to his right have any.

A swishing noise came from somewhere in the art room. Jackie stepped out of the kiln room and saw the potter's wheel spinning.

He hurried out of the room then went to the northeast stairway. Still quiet. Maybe the activities were done for the day.

He crept up the stairs to the main level and listened for sounds of Mr. Martin. All was quiet, so it would be much easier to sneak about the school, especially during the day. He distracted himself from the creepiness of the Art room and thought about how he skipped Miss Stilwell's session today. He knew he shouldn't have, but it wasn't like he was gone long and she didn't have to go looking for him. But then, now he had a reason to return to her class.

On the first floor, he tiptoed down the long, narrow side hallway. When he passed the gym entrance, he heard a soft knock in there and peeked into the dimness. What a creepy place it was when no one was around. He went on down the hall, past Miss Little's classroom, went to the main hallway, past that accident location to the main stairway. Up the stairs he went, to the second-floor main hallway. And there was Miss Stilwell's room, door closed. He picked the lock like he had before and went in, closing the door behind him. An object on Miss Stilwell's desk glinted in the quiet afternoon sun. Her desk was mostly clear except for papers and the shiny object.

What is that! Before, when he left, he thought a key was sitting there. But this, this looked fascinating. He went and picked it up. It was rectangular, thin and looked like it was made of silver. So he stashed it in his pocket and turned for a fast exit. As he approached the door, a draft brushed past him. He reached for the doorknob and twisted it. Locked. Time for the hairpin. He tried and it clicked differently this time; he couldn't unlock it. He tried again, and again, but couldn't pick the lock. After a minute of frantic trying, no luck. He was trapped.

Distant footsteps in the hall. They drew louder, closer. They stopped outside the door. Jackie took a deep breath as the lock clicked as someone inserted a key. The door opened and he jumped back.

"Well, Jackie," said Miss Stilwell, "I'm glad you're back. You have an amazing talent for getting into places. You have a bright future in jail for breaking and entering." She went to her desk and looked around it. "And jail time for theft. Is that your plan for life? Now, take a seat, young man."

He sat and Maggie handed him a paper with questions. "We're not leaving until you answer all these in a row correctly out loud. We'll go through them first, then I'll read them to you, starting with the first. If you answer correctly, I'll read the next question. Answer that one correctly, we go to the next, and so on. As we go through all thirty questions, if you miss one, we start over and go again until you miss, and start over again. We do this until you get all thirty in a row correct. Then you may leave. Understand? But first, I'd like my card holder back now."

He returned it to her and they spent the rest of the afternoon going through the questions.

June 10, 1918

Maggie

After Jackie left and Maggie locked up, she went downstairs, gripping the card holder as she stepped into the first-floor main hallway. She sighed and strolled over to the accident scene, rotating the card holder in her hand as she went to the spot.

"Thank you for this, Ricky. I'll cherish it forever. I know you can't hear me, but it helps if I talk to you here. Even though you're gone, your past mind spoke directly to me when I received this card holder and what a feeling that was. I am honored that you thought of me like that. I only wish you could have known of my appreciation."

She started to stroll around, looking for anyone present in the shadowy hallways.

"I want to confess something," she continued, listening to the soft echoes of her voice bounce off the walls between footsteps. "Something on my mind for weeks.

"Ricky, when a friend like you dies, it's a shock to hear of it. One is sad and eventually, one goes on with life. But this is different. I try to continue on. I have my work and my friends, and my students, but I've been growing fonder of you, even though you're gone. Fond of your memory and fond of what might have been. I think it's that—fond of what might have been. It's strange, I know. The more I think of you, the more you are a very special friend. I worry that it's not normal to think like this, but who's to say what's normal for this, you know?

"What might have been, indeed. I have another confession. Would your terrible accident have happened if we had gotten to know each other? I mean, because circumstances could have been different? I read once about how one thing can set the course of future events. Even though it's impossible to know if it'd been different, I'll always regret not getting to know you. Should I have been more forward? Some think it's not ladylike, but I don't know how much I agree with that and sometimes I think it's a confining concept. You probably didn't know that about me, but I imagine you would have been open to that. Then again, maybe that's just me conjuring up a part of your persona that I might have wished. Maybe I should have approached you more? I had hoped my little waves in front of your rooming house were enough to get you to approach me. I miss your little smiles from the porch. And what about that night after the play? What *were* you going to say?

"That's all I have to say for now, Ricky. I need to go home so I'll say goodbye now and I'll talk to you again."

Maggie went to the north exit and left the building.

She headed up the sidewalk to Third Street and took her time walking home. The cicadas were starting to sing while cottonwood tree seeds floated everywhere, settling onto people's yards like snow. As she walked down the small hill along Third Street toward downtown, a Model T driven by Ricky's friend Benny came by and slowed to a stop.

He leaned out and said, "Say, good-looking you need a ride?"

Maggie went up to him. "I don't know, sir. It's not proper to get into a car with just anyone."

He laughed. "It's all right. Get in. I'll take you home."

She stepped onto the running board and climbed in. "Whose home?" she asked. "I'm not that kind of…"

"I was thinking we could have coffee."

"That's a nice offer, but thank you, no. Maybe later."

"All right, I'll drop you off at the Oxford. Maybe we could have a picnic sometime with some of your friends."

"I'll think about that," she said.

June 15, 1918

The Royal Café, Main Street

Rose took a seat by herself at one of the fancy linen-draped tables in the Ladies Parlor at the Royal Café where she would meet Maggie. Two of her acquaintances, Abby and Doris sat a nearby table, carrying on a conversation Rose couldn't avoid overhearing. She glanced at them occasionally.

Doris took a bite from her sandwich and reached across the table to tap the back of Abby's hand. "I'm worried about her, aren't you?" she asked.

Abby nodded. "I am a little. I guess she's doing all right, but I don't know."

"She's not normal," Doris said. "What about that obsession? And she's teaching our kids."

"Yes," Abby said. "Obsessed with someone we never saw her with."

Doris snickered. "Maybe we just didn't see them together, or maybe they shared a bed."

Abby shrugged. "Who knows? She's probably all right. I haven't noticed her moping around. Maybe she's just keeping his memory alive in her mind. At least somebody is." She took hold of the four-leaf clover pendant that she wore on a chain around her neck and brought it to her lips. "Wishing good luck for her."

Doris took a bite of soup, then said, "Maybe we could introduce her to a nice gentleman."

"A couple come to mind," said Abby.

"Who? That George Fielding fellow?"

Abby shook her head. "Married."

"Benny Hodges then?" suggested Doris.

"Maybe. He's fairly nice, but a bit of a loudmouth."

Doris sighed. "Handsome, though."

Abby shook her head. "That's not what she needs."

"Or maybe she needs somebody who's dead," Doris said.

Abby giggled. "She already has that."

"You're right," Doris said. "She doesn't need two dead men fighting over her."

Rose had enough, got up, and went to their table.

Doris and Abby looked up.

"Why hello, Rosie," Doris said. "Would you like to join us?"

"Yes, thank you," said Rose as she took a seat at the table. "Say, ladies, I didn't mean to eavesdrop, but you should be careful."

"You're right, of course," said Abby. "We should be careful that people don't notice us talking about her."

"Except for you overhearing us, Rose," Doris said, "I'm sure we've kept it to ourselves."

"I'm not taking about other people," said Rose. She glanced at Abby's pendant, looked around the room and up above. "I'm talking about that hex."

"Hex?" asked Abby.

"That young man who died in the construction accident. He liked Maggie and any gossiping about her awakens his ire."

Abby drew a deep breath. She and Doris got up to leave after a minute and Rose could barely contain her laughter before they left the room.

* * *

Maggie held her parasol up against the unrelenting sun. As she walked down Main Street, she glanced up at the long, red-brick Opera House building's ornate moulding that ran along its upper façade.

"I think of you, Ricky," she said aloud, "every time I look at different architectural styles of our downtown buildings. No doubt you found this building interesting as well as our other buildings. I would have liked a walking tour with you pointing out the different kinds of architecture."

She took the card holder out and gazed at it. "Richard Austin, Architect."

Abby and Doris came out of the Royal Café just ahead. Maggie walked to them.

"Oh, Maggie, dear," Abby said. "How *are* you? We don't see enough of each other. Let's meet for ice cream sometime. We'd love to get together, wouldn't we, Doris?"

Maggie thought she noticed Doris rolling her eyes.

"Yes, let's," Doris said.

"Of course," said Maggie, "I'd love to. Would you like to join Rose and me in here now?"

"We just finished," Doris said. "Rose is there now."

"Thank you," said Maggie.

Abby kissed Maggie's cheek. "Till next time."

Mr. Gray, the proprietor, greeted Maggie. "Welcome, Miss Stilwell. Someone is waiting for you in the Ladies Parlor, the only one in town, I always say."

"I've seen your ads," said Maggie, smiling. "That sounds very nice."

"You can order anything from our lunch menu." He led her through a door to where Rose sat.

Rose smiled. "Hi, Maggie, how are you?"

"I just had an interesting encounter with Abby and Doris outside, but I'm doing fine considering this heat. We need rain. I'm working with some summer session students, you know. One has been a challenge, but I think he's coming around. I still have more free time than during the school year so that's been nice."

"I mean, how are you doing concerning Ricky?"

Maggie placed the card holder onto the table.

Rose got a puzzled look and Maggie explained it to her.

"That's so. . .unexpected," said Rose. "How pretty. Who would've thought?"

"It sure caught me by surprise."

"Please excuse me for asking, but—and I'm sorry to say this—is it time to move on with your life?"

"I know it's not normal since we were really just acquaintances, but I just keep thinking of him."

"Would you be deterred by another gentleman?"

"Possibly."

"Well," said Rose, "I ran into Benny Hodges and he mentioned something about having a picnic with us."

"He asked me, too. I told him I'd think about it. Any other fellows with him?"

"Oh, no, he would want all the ladies to himself."

Maggie laughed. "And then we draw straws?"

"Probably. The winner doesn't get him, right?"

"Right." Maggie said, laughing.

June 29, 1918

Ricky

I am roaming the halls this evening, contemplating things while the rain patters outside. It's the first rain in Eureka since late May and I hope it brings relief to the farmers for their crops and livestock, not to mention other people and living things. Living things, indeed. I'm still getting used to this realm I'm in.

It's darker than it usually is during the early evening in June. The clouds must be pretty thick. There's not much wind and there's just occasional lightning, so I wonder if this is enough rain to ease the drought.

I pace up and down the second-floor main hallway as I often do. There's a long radiator by the wall opposite the lockers. I missed being on the crew to install the radiators. The plumbers completed most of the work before I was able to apply. I probably wouldn't have had to climb scaffolding for that kind of work except for the plumbing work in the ceilings below the floors. If only I had left the oil rig sooner. If only I had tried to court Maggie. If only I could go back and do those…but time doesn't work that way and there's no indication that it's any different in this strange realm. I appreciated Maggie's thoughts a couple or three weeks ago and I'm glad she likes the card holder. I *was* speaking directly to her when I asked Clyde to give it to her if *this* happened. Another 'if only': if only I had given the card holder to her myself when I could.

I mosey along and reach the front stairway area. The gray rain pounds against the tall windows above the landing. Distant lightning flashes, flickering around the hallways.

I continue south down the wide hallway and go by the history classroom. After that, the corridor becomes a hall of teacher portraits, some who taught in Eastside Grade School. They'd be hard for people to see in the typical low light here, especially like today. Mr. Martin should install lighting fixtures on the portraits like in museums.

The first portrait has the caption, "Miss Julia Gould, Third & Fourth Grades, Eastside Grade School 1903." She encouraged my interest in construction and architecture before my folks moved us back to El Dorado.

Sorry, Miss Gould that your efforts teaching me were in vain.

On down the hallway, I proceed to the shadowy end wall to a portrait of a woman. It's hanging crooked. I read the caption, "Miss Mary Service, Principal, Eastside Grade School and Greenwood County Superintendent, 1914–1917." I straighten her picture, and then I look into her eyes and feel the authority of her look. It's like she's looking past me to any student who views her portrait.

A lightning strike flashes through the halls and a reflection in the glass catches my attention, the flash illuminating a hazy smudge outside Maggie's door. I step away from the portrait, stroll by the other portraits, and amble back north along the hallway. I pass the main stairway. In a lightning strike illumination, the hazy smudge pops over to the top of the north stairs and drops from view. If I had eyes, I would rub them. Continuing on, I go past the

91

lockers, past Maggie's door, get to the north stairs and look around. Nothing there.

I decide to go down to the first floor. The lightning strikes continue, flashing around the otherwise dim hallways. I decide to go to the south end and go down that side hall. When I reach the gym entrance near the stage, I go in and walk around in the middle. The gym is darker than it usually is at this time on a Saturday after the summer gymnasts and coaches have gone home. Lightning keeps flashing. It's very quiet in here except for muffled thunder. I exit the gym into the main hallway and walk by my accident scene. It's been over four months. I stroll toward the front stairway and ascend the stairs. The storm outside tapers off and the rain and lightning end. I poke around the second floor and the side hallways during the dark quiet. I walk the dusky south hallway back toward the hall of portraits. How many students have they all taught?

When I pass the portrait of Mary Service that I straightened, I glance over at Miss Gould's.

Now *her* portrait is crooked.

July 8, 1918

Carolyn

Carolyn stepped onto the screened-in back porch of her house and skipped down the steps to the patio. She was early, but the heat of the day was already bearing down. She wanted to meet Marcia before summer gymnastics started later this morning, so she skipped through the neighboring backyards and crossed Maple Street and an open grassy area to the railroad tracks where she balanced herself walking along a rail until a train's far-off whistle reminded her to hop off there. Time to go meet Marcia anyway.

She ran to the school's southeast entrance, went in, wiped perspiration from her forehead, and went down the hall toward the main hallway where Marcia said she would be and waited by the stairway. Noises in the gym signaled the arrival of someone, a coach or another girl. Carolyn went to the gym entrance and looked in. No one was visible yet so she stepped in and glanced around. The side horse sat over near a wall with the uneven bars and appeared to have been fixed. She crept over to the equipment and ran her hand across the side horse leather and took hold of the handles to test how secure they were. They didn't budge. Next, she went to the uneven bars and grabbed one of the bars. She was tempted to pull herself up and try a routine she had learned, but decided not to without spotters there. There was a small table with chair near the adjacent wall. She went to the table and pulled a sheet of paper from a stack that Miss Jones must have left there. They had hand-copied large letters: "DON'T GIVE UP."

It was fun having the gym to herself but kind of eerie and she had heard stories; She held onto the paper and started to wander around the basketball court. She tiptoed through the middle and felt the silence and when walking toward the stage, a bump downstage startled her. She stopped walking and peeked into the shadows behind the curtains. Marcia was playing a trick on her. She pulled herself onto the stage.

"All right, Marcia," she said. "Stop this!" Then she noticed a piano sitting to the side beneath a dust cover and started to go to it.

Carolyn!

It sounded like Marcia was out in the main hall.

Carolyn hopped off the stage and ran the length of the gym to the far end, to the exit. As she stepped into the hallway, she glanced back in toward the stage. The curtains were waving.

Carolyn!

Marcia was somewhere out here in the hall. What a relief!

"I'm here!" Carolyn shouted.

Marcia didn't reply. All was still after Carolyn's echo faded.

"Marcia? You out here somewhere?"

Carolyn!

Upstairs.

Carolyn climbed the main stairs and went north along the lockers.

"Marcia! Where are you?" she shouted.

No reply. Still playing tricks on her, so Carolyn walked up and down the hallway past the main stairway and the portraits caught her eye. She had always been in a hurry when changing classes during school and had never looked closely at the portraits. One of the portraits was crooked so she straightened it and went to study each picture then looked at the paper she carried. "Don't give up," she whispered. "Right, ladies? You didn't."

She stood out in the middle and looked around at them. They were an inspiration.

Carolyn!

This time the voice was over by the north stairs near Miss Stilwell's classroom.

"Marcia, where are you! Stay put and stop trying to frighten me!"

She headed toward the north stairs. When she reached the area, Marcia wasn't there and a breeze wafted by snatching the sheet of paper from her hand. Somebody-Something played scales on the piano down on the stage.

Goosebumps covered her arms and legs. She briskly walked backwards along the hallway, watching the paper float about as it zigzagged from wall to wall until it settled onto the floor in front of Miss Stilwell's classroom and slid under the door.

Carolyn rushed downstairs to the front doors out to the front walk. She looked for Marcia, but couldn't spot her anywhere so she went around the school building to Third Street, over to Maple Street where she headed toward the high school. At Fourth Street, she walked diagonally across grounds of Eureka High. Some boys were playing baseball on the east side of the building. Here on the west side, the nearly overhead sun was beating down onto the front sidewalk and red bricks of the building, a large place where she would attend high school the next school year. The thought of that caused butterflies in her stomach. She sat on the front steps and scooted next to the doors into a small shadow.

Birds chirped in the heat as if they didn't care. Carolyn took a deep breath and tried to forget the strangeness in Mulberry School. She didn't know whether to go back and see if they started gymnastics, but she wanted to find Marcia. She was thirsty and decided to go downtown first and get a bottle of pop.

When she arrived at West 3rd Street Grocery, Mr. Mack greeted her.

"You look flushed, young lady. Go to the ice box and get yourself a bottle of Coca-Cola. What brings you around, Carolyn?"

"Just thirsty. I'm going to the school to start summer gymnastics."

"It's a hot one today, so you'd better get going. I think your friend Marcia is there waiting for you. She came in a while ago."

Carolyn went to Mulberry School and Marcia was sitting on the front steps.

"Where were you?" she said to Carolyn.

"I was here," Carolyn said, "where were you?"

July 10, 1918

Maggie

A couple of days later, Maggie arrived at the school. The weather had cooled down a bit since Monday and she otherwise would have been doing something outside in the mild weather this afternoon, but she had to get caught up on work with her summer session students and she had papers to grade.

As she reached her room, Mr. Martin met her at the door.

"Good afternoon, Miss Stilwell."

Hello, Mr. Martin, what's new?"

He held up a sheet of paper with writing. "I found this on the floor inside your door yesterday and put it on your desk, but a draft must have blown it off your desk later."

"Thank you," she said as he handed it to her.

"I'll get back to my rounds then," he said as he went back out to the hallway.

She sat at her desk and looked at the paper. "DON'T GIVE UP." She put it aside for now and started to grade papers. It looked like one student hadn't read the assignments, which was a shame, because she knew he was a bright kid. She wondered if she had failed to inspire him or help him get interested in the subject matter. Most of her students enjoyed the class this school year so she wondered if this boy just had an issue with focusing on his work. She could relate to that, but one had to push through that if possible and he needed help.

After several hours of finishing the papers, she recorded the grades, then put the gradebook safely in her desk and locked the drawer. She got her things together and left her room.

On her way to the accident location, she thought about the message on the sheet of paper, and when she got there, several papers floated on a draft out from the gym and settled on the hallway floor in a scattered pile.

She gathered them up. "Oh, these are Miss Jones's," she said. She straightened them and took the stack into gym to the little table and looked for something to use for a paperweight. Not finding anything, she went to a small wheeled chalkboard and took the box of chalk and eraser and used them for paperweights, then went back to the hallway, to the accident location.

"Well, Ricky," she said. "It's been a while. The message on that paper, 'Don't give up' is interesting, isn't it? It could be applied to Jackie Vincent for me not to give up on him and help him move along with school. I know he can do it. I don't know what else that message tells me. Abby would insist it's a 'sign' or something, but I don't usually jump to such a conclusion. Some might say it's telling me not to give up on you. But it's not necessary, because I have no intention of forgetting you or not keeping your memory alive. I still wonder about what-ifs and probably will for some time. I want you to know your memory is worthy of preserving."

September 4, 1918

Annie

Hammering in the hallway outside the library gave Annie Marsh a start. She leaned out the door. The carpenter was on his knees nailing floor trim into place along the wall.

"Ah, hello, ma'am," he said. "I'm just reinstalling the trim. The original was getting loose and the boss wants it fixed. It's not just to make it look nicer, which it should in a brand-new school, but we're doing some last-minute fixing of things for the new school year. I'll be finished here in about thirty minutes after I work on the crown moulding along the ceiling before doing the next section."

"Thank you," said Annie. "It's rattling the bookshelves." And my nerves, she thought.

She went back into the library and checked the shelves. The books were secure in their places and she resumed her work as more hammering came from the hall's ceiling area. She tried to ignore the racket and went through more books still to be shelved.

An abrupt stop to the noise a while later was a relief and the eerie quiet of the empty school returned when the worker left the building, his closing of a distant door echoing throughout. After she finished shelving books, she decided to take an opportunity to explore the empty school.

She went down to the main hallway where sunlight draped across the floor onto the wall. Two doors on the right opened into the upper gallery of the gym. Annie walked through the first door and went a few steps down to where she could gaze at the mostly dark gym below. Dim light spilled in through the exits below. Annie gasped at movement near the stage. She crouched and peered at the area. All was still. Then she heard whispering. Goosebumps covered her arms. More sounds from there: She suppressed a laugh when she heard kissing noises. She had wanted to go down to the main floor of the gym, but wasn't sure now. Then again…

She stood. "Hello down there!"

"Oh!" came a quick response followed by fast footsteps and two figures running toward the front exits.

Annie chuckled, went back out to the main hall and made her way down to the first floor. A young couple dashed out the gym door and ran past her toward the front doors.

Annie started to enter the gym. "How about if I go to the scene of the crime," she muttered. When she reached the stage, she went along it, sliding her hand on it as a guide in the dark. About halfway along, she kicked something and almost tripped: a purse.

She picked the purse up and went back out to the main hallway. She started to open it and was met by a teenager running in from outside toward her.

The girl stopped, out of breath. "Please, may I have my purse?"

Annie handed it to her. "You broke the rules," she said. "Do I need to report you?"

"Oh, please, we won't come in here again!"

"Running in the hall is against the rules," said Annie.

The girl released a nervous laugh, thanked Annie and left to rejoin the other.

"Wow," said Annie aloud, "you never know what you'll encounter in this new school."

She went back up to the library and prepared to go home.

September 9, 1918

Annie

The following Monday, Annie was in the library early, looking through a stack of old copies of *The Eureka Herald* and *Democratic Messenger* weekly newspapers for an article, something she remembered reading the year before. After a while, she found it. "Eureka!" she said.

An article in the June 14, 1917 *Messenger* said: "Work commenced on the new grade school Monday morning. The work will be pushed as rapidly as possible. It is hoped to have the building ready for occupancy by January 1st."

"Well," she muttered, "we didn't make the January first date and then we lost poor Ricky Austin…"

She put the newspapers away and started to get ready for the first day of school. A little later, students started entering the building. Some commotion and laughter in the hallway drew her to the door. A primary school boy ran toward her and tripped, marbles flying out and bouncing around.

Annie stood in front of him. "What's the matter with you! You walk straight to your class now."

The boy gathered the marbles into his pockets and went down the hall looking as if walking instead of running took some effort.

Back in the library, Annie went to the bookcases and straightened some recently shelved books. After finishing the east wall, she started on the north shelf. The books there looked fine except for a couple. She reached up for

102

one book and her foot slipped on something sending her stumbling backwards a few feet from the bookshelf.

The long bulletin board from above the bookcase crashed to the floor in front of her.

She sat up and two teachers rushed in. "Are you all right?" asked one.

The other offered her hand and helped Annie up.

"Look," said the first, holding up a large marble.

"Oh my goodness!" said Annie. "Phew! I didn't think any marbles rolled in here! It must have ricocheted in."

"Where did it come from?"

"It's the little Higgins boy's. He was running in the hall and tripped."

"If you hadn't slipped back on that marble, that bulletin board would have hit you."

September 9, 1918

Miss Owens

That same Monday, around 8:00AM, Miss Owens entered her Second Grade classroom on the west side of the first-floor hallway and started putting her things away. She always kept a ruler on her desk and noticed it missing. In fact, her desk looked like it had been rearranged, not only was her ruler missing, so was the switch she kept next to it. She looked in the wastebasket under the desk only to find a crumpled dunce cap at the bottom.

She shrugged and would speak to Mr. Martin about it. Young voices in the hallways meant students arriving for the day.

Josh Higgins arrived first, catching his breath as he walked in the door.

"Why are you panting, young man?" she asked him. "Were you running in the hall?"

"Um, yeah. Miss Marsh caught me and told me to walk to class so I did."

"She should have done more than that. Why, you'd have gotten my switch to your behind if I'd caught you. Now get to your desk and remain still until class starts."

"But I have to go to the restroom."

"Well, you can wait," she said, pointing to his desk.

Josh sat and held onto himself, trying to prevent an embarrassing accident. Miss Owens went to the door and waited for her approaching students. She started to step into the hall and tripped over something she didn't see, causing a commotion of students and other teachers when she landed on the floor.

Linda Hendricks assisted her, helping her sit up.

When Miss Owens was facing away, Josh sneaked out and hurried down to the restroom. He returned when a group of students started to line up outside the class and went in with them.

Miss Owens entered the class after them. She faced the gawking students. "Take your seats!"

They scrambled to sit while she went to her desk and sat. She took out a small piece of paper and wrote something on it.

"Josh, you seem to like going around in the halls. Take this note down to Mr. Martin. I want him to look at that floor where I fell. And don't you stop at a restroom or a drinking fountain on the way or do any running. If you walk down and deliver this note, you'll be back by the time class starts."

"By myself?" he said. "It's scary down there."

"Of course, by yourself. Now take this note and get going, you big baby."

Josh went down the hall to the northeast stairway. He skipped down the stairs to the basement's main hallway outside of the Art classroom. Mr. Martin emerged from the far side of the hall and Josh skipped over to him.

"Whoa there, young fella," Mr. Martin said. "What are you doing down here now?"

"Miss Owens told me to bring this note to you."

Mr. Martin looked at it and mumbled, "There ain't anything wrong with that floor."

"Miss Owens tripped and fell there."

"Hmmm. Well, all right. Come on. I'll take you up there."

They reached the second-grade classroom and Josh went in to his desk.

Miss Owens went to Mr. Martin in the hall and started talking about the floor where she tripped.

"I'll have a look if you'll permit me."

She stepped back and he got on his knees. He rubbed his hand across the floor. "Nothing there," he said. He got low and eyeballed it.

Miss Owens went back in the classroom.

Mr. Martin stood. "I didn't see anything."

"I'm glad you didn't," she said.

"I'll bring my level on my rounds and check for unevenness." He left and went back to her desk. Josh looked over at Violet, who was wiping tears away. He wanted to ask her what was wrong.

When she let out a whimper, Miss Owens said, "Why are you crying? Stop it."

"I don't feel well."

"Well, sit still for a while and stay quiet. Class, take out your readers. Go to page four."

The students complied and Miss Owens went to stand over Sharon.

"Sharon," she said, "start reading."

Sharon put her finger on the page. "Pop has dat hat," she said.

"Read it again. 'Pop has *that* hat.'"

Sharon took a deep breath. "Pop has dat hat."

"No," Miss Owens said. "It's 'that', not 'dat'. Say it."

"Dat," Sharon said.

"It's not dat!" Say 'that'!"

"Dat."

Miss Owens grabbed Sharon's shoulders and shook her. "Say 'that'! It's not dat! Say it!"

"Dat."

Miss Owens shook her again. Sharon started crying.

"Learn how to say it!"

"I'm trying." She continued to cry.

"All right. Go stand in the hall."

Sharon got up and went out, whimpering for the next few minutes.

After a bit, Miss Owens went out to the hall to Sharon.

"Have you learned your lesson? Say 'that'."

That! Miss Owens thought she heard.

"Much better. It sounded far away. Did you have your hand over your mouth?"

"No," Sharon said, nor had she said or heard anything.

September 28, 1918

Superstitious

"You won't get over your superstitions if you don't face up to them," Doris said as she and Abby walked along Mulberry Street toward the school. "There's nothing going on in there no matter what you've heard. I'm going to show you the silliness of the whole idea when we go in and you observe nothing strange is happening. The only strange thing in here ever is Maggie talking to her dead friend."

Abby rubbed the clover leaf pendant between her fingers. "I don't want you to. There's nothing wrong with being superstitious. And by the way, we haven't spoken kindly of Maggie." Abby brought the pendant to her chin.

"She needs something to snap her out of her strange behavior," Doris said.

"I don't see her behaving differently than before if perhaps not as perky as she used to be," Abby said. "Mourning a friend like that isn't unheard of. Her busy schedule with school in session probably keeps her going."

"Maybe," Doris said. "I bet that obsession still has a hold on her. And look at you cuddling that clover leaf as if it's got some hold on you."

"I've had this since grade school."

Doris laughed.

"I can tell you some stories," Abby said.

"I'll bet you can. I'm going to take that silly thing from you before we go in."

Abby held a tight grip on it. "No."

They continued along the sidewalk toward the school, Abby holding onto the pedant as they took the front sidewalk toward the entrance. "We're actually going in?" she said.

"Of course we are," Doris said, pointing to a Model T parked along the street. "Looks like Mr. Martin's working today so it should be open."

Abby looked up at the tall windows above the double doors as they reached the entrance. Doris opened one of the doors. "See, it's open," she said, ushering Abby in.

Abby, hesitant as she entered, pointed ahead. "Is that where that poor guy fell?"

Doris shrugged. "I think so." She pointed to the ceiling. "All the way from there."

"Oh my!" Abby said as she started to walk over to the accident location.

"Wait!" Doris said, grabbing her arm.

"What!"

"The floor is wet."

"Oh! Thank you!" Abby said, rubbing the clover leaf. "I could have thrown my hip out slipping on that."

"Come on, let's go," Doris said.

"Where? I thought we were here to observe this spot."

"No, let's walk around."

Doris led Abby to the stairway and they went up to the second floor.

Up there, they went into one of the upper gallery entrances above the gym.

Doris pointed down to the dark gym. "We should go down there and stay for a while," she said.

"What for?"

"To wait for anything strange to happen, which it won't."

A knock from below startled them.

"Mr. Martin," Doris said.

Abby saw movement in the dark. "Did you see that?"

"As I just said, it's Mr. Martin."

"Then why don't we ask him if he's noticed anything strange?"

Doris shook her head. "He hasn't."

"How do you know?" Abby asked, looking down at the dark expanse.

"Because nothing strange has happened. Come on." Doris led Abby back out to the hallway and they strolled past Maggie's class and down the side hall to the northeast stairway at the end. When they reached it, Doris gripped the wood handrail and started to step down, but slid forward as her hand slipped down the rail. She caught herself and Abby helped her back up to the top.

"Too much oil on the railing," Doris said, shaking her hand.

"Maybe Mr. Martin's doing something with it," said Abby. "He's not expecting anyone here."

"That's right," Doris said. "I should have been careful. Let's go back to the main hallway."

They went back and continued to stroll around the wide hall toward the south end to the hall of portraits area.

"Who are these people?" asked Abby.

"Teachers. Most of them taught at Eastside School some years before it burned."

"Are they all still alive?"

"They're all still around. A couple are teaching here and several are now at Walnut and Northside schools."

"That's nice to have their portraits on display like this," Abby said.

"Now you can stay and read all about them," Doris said.

Abby looked around. "What do you mean? You're going to leave me alone here?"

Doris nodded. "You're going to spend a little time here by yourself and see there's nothing strange about being alone here in the school. Don't worry, these teachers will keep you company."

"Where are you going?" Abby asked.

"For a walk around the school. I missed the dedication in March." Doris winked and walked away.

"Don't be long," Abby mumbled.

Doris didn't answer and continued on.

Abby kept hold of her clover leaf and went to the first portrait to read about Miss Gould. She tried to ignore the feeling that the portraits were watching her, took a deep breath, then went along the wall and read the captions on the other portraits. Miss Mary Service was interesting: A teacher, a principal, and superintendent. Abby stepped away from it and stood in the middle of the hallway.

The quiet permeated her.

"You're all very accomplished," she said aloud. "I don't know that I could do what you do. Maybe I could, but it takes someone special like each of you to teach young people who'll be leaders of tomorrow. I hope they all come to appreciate you one day."

Pacing around a little, she continued talking. "Where is Doris? Leaving me alone like this. Maybe it's all right. I'm doing fine." She looked around at the portraits again and smiled. "Aren't I doing fine, ladies?"

Knocking sounds from the gym gallery entrance gave her a start. She crept over to it and peeked in. All was still except for slight knocks and thumps down in the darkness. It was unnerving, so she stepped back to the hallway.

Some commotion came from the south hall. Abby went over there and stared down to the end. It was still except for more distant knocks and thuds coming from the far stairway.

Then footsteps from there caused her to jump. They grew frantic, louder, closer. Goosebumps rose on her arms, back, and neck.

Then Doris jumped up from the far stairway. She ran toward Abby, almost knocking her over.

Out of breath, she said, "Abby, I'm glad you're still here!"

"What!" Abby took Doris's hand and felt her trembling.

"Let's get out of here!" Doris blurted out.

Abby led Doris to the front stairs, down to the landing. Doris stopped and caught her breath. "Oh dear," she said.

"What is it, Doris?"

"Let's go—please!" Doris said, pointing down the stairs.

They went down to the main entrance. Doris grabbed Abby's hand and pulled her outside.

On the steps, Doris let go of Abby, ran to the curb, and pointed to the Model T parked on the street.

"That's not Mr. Martin's car!" she shouted. "No one's in the school!"

October 11, 1918

Maggie

The new closing proclamation for schools and other gathering places was extended to October 21st due to the influenza epidemic, and Maggie still had to work on lesson plans for when school reopened, so she decided to go up to Mulberry this afternoon. She walked up the small hill amid yellow leaves floating down from the fall foliage above; she looked forward to piles of fallen leaves in the coming weeks and the smells of autumn.

She reached Mulberry Street on the hilltop and strolled toward the school, enjoying the warm autumn day and the light fog for which the rain the day before was responsible. She could see the outline of Mr. Martin's old pickup parked along Second Street on the south side of the school grounds. She continued on to the front doors. Once inside, she headed to her classroom.

"Well," she said aloud as she walked, "Ricky, what am I going to do about you? Would it have been too forward of me to approach you and settle our friendship once and for all? I'm not sure. These are modern times. It's almost the 1920s after all. We women are getting closer to the Vote in the U.S. The House passed the Nineteenth Amendment. Now it's up to that stubborn Senate in the next session after the House passes it again. In light of that, we women are getting more freedoms. Although we've got a ways to go, like Rose often says.

"I've been wondering what I should do now. Should I welcome men calling on me? People tell me to, but I ignore them because I don't feel interested, but I do try to accept that you're never coming back. It's hard. I don't want to let go of what might have been."

When she stopped talking, the quiet returned, except for knocking about noises around the building by Mr. Martin. She reached her classroom and went in, using a handkerchief on the door handle.

She set her purse and card holder on her desk next to a small stack of books and her globe. Mr. Martin was making rounds so she wanted to get ready for him and take care of anything needed in her room. She walked up and down aisles between the desks, went to the bookshelves on the back wall, and started straightening books; she paced around the room a little and went to the windows to raise one a bit to allow in the breeze. Back at the bookshelves, she knelt and arranged some bottom shelf books.

Mr. Martin was working in a nearby classroom now. She got up and left the room to go down the hall to the restroom. When she returned, Mr. Martin was sitting on the floor in the hallway outside her classroom, working on his cart.

"Hello, Mr. Martin," she said, stepping toward her door. "Is everything all right?"

"I'll be in in a minute or two as soon as I fix this wheel," he said, continuing to work on it.

She went in to her desk and when she started to gather her things, she noticed her card holder was missing.

A check of the desk, the books and globe revealed no card holder.

She checked near the bookshelves and went to the windows. She didn't find it so she went to the hallway and glanced down the to see if she noticed an object on the floor.

Mr. Martin looked up at her. "What's the matter, Miss Stilwell?"

"Oh, it's nothing. I think I dropped something, but it's not out here."

She went back in to the desk and looked around its surface again, under her purse, and checked the floor. She didn't find it there, so she sat and fished around in the wastebasket.

There it was—amid discarded items. She grabbed it, let out a sigh, put it in her purse, and stood.

Mr. Martin entered the room with his cart working now.

"I would have been finished in here by now," he said, heading to her desk to grab the wastebasket. "I never had trouble with that wheel before." He emptied the wastebasket into the cart.

Maggie smiled. "I'm glad you were delayed this time."

October 31, 1918

Maggie

On a warm, sunny Halloween afternoon, Mr. Gray emerged from the Royal Café holding two dishes of ice cream and handed them to Maggie and Rose. "You may take these up to the gazebo and enjoy," he said.

They thanked him and hurried toward the courthouse grounds to get to the gazebo before the ice cream melted.

"Wait, there's a young couple in the gazebo," said Rose. "Let's not bother them."

They went and sat on the courthouse steps.

"I hate how this epidemic has changed so many things this year, what with restaurants and so many places having to close," said Maggie, taking a bite of ice cream. "Not to mention the poor souls who've lost their lives right here in Eureka, as well as some of our brave soldiers. Yet look at us enjoying ice cream this afternoon when I would normally be at school teaching if they hadn't extended the closing order."

"We don't need to feel guilty," said Rose. "Especially you."

"Why, today I would be welcoming the grade school students touring the junior high classrooms to show off their costumes. Some of those kids were so imaginative with their costumes before. Last year, the grade school teachers brought their kids over to my eighth-grade class at the high school. One fourth grade boy was dressed in old rags made to look like bandages with red paint like he was badly injured. I asked him how he came up with that idea and he said his mother did, that she opposed our entry into the War and wanted to show what war was."

"You've not had it easy this year, with Ricky's fall."

"I am managing."

"Are you still thinking of him?"

"Always." Maggie stirred her melting ice cream. "In fact, I talk to him whenever I can."

Rose drew back a bit. "You don't."

Chuckling, Maggie said, "I didn't mean he talks back to me. I just say things out loud that I wish he could hear."

"Oh, well then, I was thinking you were having séances."

"No," said Maggie, "but maybe Abby has ideas about that."

"I doubt it," said Rose. She stood and picked up their dishes. "I'll return these to Mr. Gray," she said, turning to the café.

Maggie thanked her and went to the sidewalk. The autumn weather felt nice as she strolled along Main Street to the Oxford and met Mrs. Thrall in the rooming house's living room who handed her a letter. "This came for you today."

Maggie regarded the return address. It was from Clyde and Marie Austin in El Dorado. She puzzled over what this could be and went to sit on the sofa.

"I have fresh tea made," Mrs. Thrall said. "I'll bring you a cup with lemon and sugar."

Maggie thanked her, opened the envelope, and pulled out a letter along with a second sealed envelope containing another letter.

She unfolded the first.

October 20, 1918

Dear Maggie,

We were remiss in not forwarding this letter to you before now. It was with Ricky's personal effects that we sorted through a month or so after we saw you in May.

Yours faithfully,
Clyde and Marie Austin
El Dorado, Kansas

Mrs. Thrall returned with a cup and saucer and placed them onto the small coffee table in front of Maggie.

Maggie waited to sip her tea and opened the sealed letter with shaky hands, careful not to rip it in her haste.

February 18, 1918

Dear Maggie,
I asked my cousin Clyde, and Marie, to give my silver card holder to you if anything ever happens to me. I certainly do not expect anything will and my hope is that I will someday get to know you better, to ask your permission to court you if I ever get up the nerve. I do not know if I am worthy of you, but I can only hope to convince you that I am. Your morning waves fill me with warm feelings, and I have friends who urge me to approach you and introduce myself, but I do not know how to do that properly. Perhaps I should write a letter

directly to you and ask to meet, but I have yet to. Writing a letter such as this one that you may never read is a way to get my thoughts down kind of like a diary, practice for when I get up the nerve to talk to you or write.

Well, my friend Benny and I are leaving this morning to work a construction job at the new grade school being built, so I will put my pen away and take my coffee to the porch and wait for your wave.

Fondly,
Ricky Austin

"Oh dear!" Maggie said, trying to remain composed. She dried the tears with her handkerchief.

Holding the letter to her chest, she rushed out of the Oxford and started walking. She strolled along Main Street while re-reading the letter, drawing subtle stares. A horn from a turning car when she was crossing Fourth Street was enough to make her put the letter away while walking, or at least watch better while crossing a street. So she stopped back at the gazebo in front of the courthouse and settled onto a bench to re-read Ricky's letter again. After a couple of reads, she got up to walk, deciding she could still talk to Ricky while walking around town so she turned west along Third Street and left downtown, walking along the tree-lined street. She looked around to see if anyone was near and started talking in a soft voice.

"Well, Ricky, your letter was well written. I didn't notice any obvious errors, except for one."

She chuckled and gazed up at the yellow foliage. "Shame on you, Ricky, for wondering if you were worthy of me. Of course you were. No question about it. Certainly worthy enough to get to know. Then we could have decided about courting, couldn't we have? And here

I go back to wondering about what might have been when I was content to keep your memory fresh. Yes, I am happy to receive your letter—your last one on that very day you left us. It's special because of that." She sighed. "Oh my."

She didn't feel the same talking to him while walking through neighborhoods as in the school, and turned back toward downtown. The school was closed today and Mr. Martin might not be there. She wandered around downtown and window shopped for a while.

As she walked by Home National Bank, a somewhat rusted old pickup pulled into the empty diagonal space and when the engine was turned off, it shook and blue smoke puffed out the tailpipe. Mr. Martin got out and went to the front of the car.

"Hello, Miss Stilwell," he said as he opened the hood's fold-out panels and started working on the engine.

"Trouble?" she said.

"I have to adjust these cables every few days to keep this thing running."

"Are you planning to go to the school today?"

"I thought about it, but I don't think so today. This thing uses so much gas, I only have enough to make a few more trips before I have to spring for more. I would walk from home, but I live pretty far away."

"I understand," she said.

He finished his work on the engine, excused himself, and went into the bank.

Maggie thought she might feel a better connection to Ricky if she went to the school and walked around the outside of the building, so she headed there. On the way, thought about the letter she was going to write to Clyde and Marie thanking them for the joy she received this afternoon.

When she reached Mulberry School, she walked around to the south grounds and gazed up at the building. The sun illuminated the upper floor rooms and she could see into the library where the sun cast light onto the bookshelves. She walked over to the building to the large stones of the foundation. She had read that some of the new foundation incorporated some of Eastside School's stones.

"Ricky," she said. "You've really got me thinking with that letter and maybe you didn't hear me earlier when I said that you shouldn't have thought you weren't worthy. How could you not have been when a letter like that from you can give me joy across time and death? That's all I have to say. I just wanted to make sure I said it here."

Sunset came earlier in October, and the school building already cast a long shadow in the low sun, stretching into the neighborhood to the east. Neighborhood kids were out playing in the cool fall evening as they often did.

* * *

Late that evening, Jackie and Andy gathered with several friends in the playground on the east side of the school.

"I brought my Ouija Board," Lisa said, holding it up. "I wish we could go trick-or-treating, but this will be fun."

"Good," said Jackie. "Where do we want to set up?"

Andy pointed to the shadowy wall of the school. "How about over there?"

"It's too dark there," said Marcia.

Jackie pulled out a candle and a small box of matches. "It's perfect," he said. "And there's no breeze tonight."

Everyone agreed and they sat and formed a circle in the dimness next to the wall and settled down. Lisa set the board up within the circle and Jackie lit his candle.

"Want to tell ghost stories first?" said Andy.

"No," said Jackie, "I want to get home after a while and study."

"What?" said Marcia.

"He is smart, but last ye—" started Andy.

Jackie cupped his hand over Andy's mouth. "Shh!"

"What?" said Lisa.

"I'm doing well in English and want to keep up."

"That's a good idea," said Marcia, "because I heard that in high school you have to read *War and Peace* twice in one week."

Jackie laughed. "No."

"I heard that, too," Lisa said.

"Never mind," Jackie said. "Let's play."

They huddled around the board and candle, their shadows dancing on the brick wall.

"Don't anybody cheat by pushing the pointer," said Andy. "Somebody always does."

"And pleeease," said Marcia, "don't make it mad."

The others laughed.

"No really!" she insisted. "My cousin said her friend picked up the pointer once and yelled at it: 'I hate you!' and threw it onto the board where it spun around in circles."

A couple of the kids gasped.

"Yeah," said Jackie, "I don't believe it."

"I've heard some things," insisted Andy.

"Who do we want to call up?" Lisa asked.

"My great uncle," said Andy.

"No," Jackie said. "We tried him before and nothing happened."

"Then who?" Marcia said.

Jackie looked up at the towering wall. "How about that guy who got killed in a fall when they were building this place?"

"My parents talk about that guy," Lisa said. "He was from out of town."

"Then can we call him up?" Marcia asked.

"Sure we can," Jackie said. "I know some guys who called up George Washington and he showed up with a cherry tree limb."

"All right," said Lisa. "What was the guy's name?"

"Richard Austin," Jackie said.

"I thought it was Ricky," said Andy.

"Same thing," Jackie said. "'Richard' was on his card—"

"His card? Andy asked.

"Never mind. All right, Ricky was his name. Lisa, it's your board. You go first."

All four put their fingers on the pointer.

Lisa looked up. "Ricky, did you love Miss Stilwell?"

"This'll be interesting," Jackie said.

"Shh," Lisa said. "My parents said he was madly in love with her."

The pointer started to twitch beneath their fingers.

"My turn," Jackie said.

"Wait," Andy said.

The pointer started sliding to "Yes."

"There, see?" Lisa said.

Then the pointer eased over to "No."

"It's not supposed to do that from one to the other," Jackie said. "Who's pushing it?"

They all took their hands away. "Not me," each one said.

Jackie put his hand back on the pointer. "Try again." The others reached back in and joined him.

"I want to ask him something," Marcia said.

"Go ahead," Jackie said.

Eric T. Reynolds

As Marcia started to say something, she jumped. "I saw something on the wall!"

"That's your shadow," Jackie said.

"It wasn't that. I saw a glow," she said.

"Come on," Jackie said, laughing. "All right then, it's my turn. Ricky, were you Miss Stilwell's secret admirer?"

The pointer nudged beneath their fingers and spelled out: "Stop that and leave."

124

October 31, 1918

Ricky

I notice kids' voices on the playground outside the stage wall.

Aww, are they having a séance?

And on Halloween night with Ouija Board and all. Wish I could participate, but I'll resist getting involved. There's that boy named Jackie exaggerating about something. I peek through the wall. They have a candle and everything looks set.

They're telling stories about weird things happening with Ouija Boards.

They sit in a circle and slide the board in place with the pointer ready for their fingers. Now they're ready to talk to the dead. They're so cute.

Uh oh, they're summoning me. Sorry—I'm not going to move your pointer. Your subconscious minds have to do it.

Aw now, Jackie just called me Richard. He must have seen that when he swiped the card holder, but I prefer Ricky. I ought to push the pointer to spell it.

"No," Andy corrects him. Well, thank you, Andy, Ricky it is.

And there it is…I figured the questions would come around to Maggie and me, with the girl asking me if I love Maggie. I expected as much with many people believing it.

No, not going to tell you. Their combined subconsciouses pushed the pointer to Yes. Wait—now they're pushing it to No.

They're arguing about who's moving the pointer. I'm not surprised, but I didn't do it.

Jackie is asking me if I was Maggie's secret admirer. Well yes, I admit it, but I'm not pushing the pointer. You kids have to figure that out.

Whoops! The girl saw me—I leaned out too far.

They're moving the pointer now. Wow—Why did they come up with *that*?

They'll think I moved it. They're leaving, scared out of their wits. And it's probably past their curfews.

At least I got to watch them. I had hoped to peek out and watch the trick-or-treaters with their costumes this evening, but not this year. Well, I guess the kids around here will talk about this day for some time, probably going down in the local lore. I don't know that I'm happy about that.

Don't you want to be remembered?

I walk away from the area and go into the long hallway that leads to the main hall.

I go up to the second floor and pace for a while along the wide hallway where I do my best thinking. First, I'll go by Maggie's door.

I enjoyed watching her walk around the school grounds today. She got the letter. Good old Clyde and Marie. I knew they wouldn't fail me. I didn't expect her reaction out on the school grounds, although I'm pleased. I feel the same way she does, a closer connection when she's inside the building. I'm always glad to see her and listen to her ruminations. Maybe she has some kind of a feeling that I listen to her, because she remains motivated to talk to me. Wishful thinking maybe, but writing that letter was a good idea.

I had to get it right the first time since there'd be no revision possible. I walk down to the portraits and gaze at the teachers, especially Miss Gould. I turn back north and walk toward Maggie's room. I wonder when the closing order will end and I get to see Maggie more.

I walk by the lockers. It was tempting to intervene in the kids' séance tonight, but I'm glad I didn't. I always try to resist interfering, but I didn't resist during that close call when Maggie found the card holder just before Mr. Martin went in to empty the trash. When I noticed Maggie frantically looking for it, I had to mess with that wheel to delay Mr. Martin going into her classroom. I figured Maggie would have been careful with something she cherishes and *something else* was the cause of it falling into the wastebasket. I have an idea about that and I intend to find out. I don't feel ashamed to have intervened that time. That was *personal*.

I wonder what Maggie has been up to lately. When school opens and she can finally come in more, I hope she continues her talks to me.

There is something going on downstairs. I go down to the first-floor hallway and stand against the wall near my accident location.

Somebody inserts a key into the front entrance doors. Two women step in.

* * *

"I probably shouldn't have brought you here."

"There are weird things happening here, Linda," Doris says. "I want a witness. What better time than on Halloween night?"

Linda walks in a few steps. "Well, we'll see, but I don't think we need to go to my classroom."

Doris creeps along behind her, looking around in the shadowy hallway lit by the ambient light of outside street lamps coming through the upper stairway windows.

Linda points ahead. "There it is."

She goes over to the accident location. "Some of us teachers feel strange here. Especially Maggie."

Doris nods. "I'm well aware of that."

"But I'm not going to dwell on her," Linda says, starting along the wall.

"I agree," Doris says. "Enough said about that. I thought about bringing my friend Abby along, but she probably wouldn't have wanted to."

They continue along the wall toward me.

"There's another one of those wall smudges," Linda says, pointing at me. "The painters paint over them and the smudges come back. Annie, the librarian swears she saw one move."

"Then I'm definitely glad I didn't bring Abby," Doris says.

I remain still, flat against the wall as they enter the gym and I follow them in.

"This gym is spooky at night," Doris says as they walk into the gloom.

"It really is. Especially the stage area."

They walk out to the middle of the gym.

"I'm glad you talked me into bringing you here," Linda says. "I've been wanting to test the acoustics again here in the gym for some time, just looking for another opportunity since Mr. Nibert caught me singing in here one morning."

"Well," Doris says, "let's hear that beautiful voice."

Linda steps away from Doris, straightens her shoulders, and takes a deep breath. In reverberating vibrato, she sings out: "Ahhhhhhh!" Her voice echoes against the walls and high ceiling, piercing the quiet.

A series of crashes upstairs cause Linda and Doris to jump. If I had most of my emotions, I would have leapt, too.

Doris grabs Linda's elbow. "Where did those crashes come from!"

"Down a hallway or upstairs."

"That's some voice you have," says Doris.

"Let's go," says Linda.

I slip along the wall and sneak out to the stairway to hurry upstairs to the second-floor to go hide behind the long radiator in the main hallway. Looking down the hall, I discover the source of the crash. Most of the teacher portraits have fallen to the floor. The portrait of Miss Gould is face down.

I wish I had time to go over and put them back up before Linda and Doris arrive up here.

November 1, 1918

Ricky

The next morning, two men are talking near the front entrance so I slip around the second-floor to the top of the front stairway and peek down.

Moments later, Principal Nibert and Police Officer Hughes start up the stairs. Time for me to go hide behind the radiator. When the two men step into the second-floor main hallway, Mr. Nibert points toward the fallen portraits at the south end of the hall.

"What some will do just for fun," he says. "I'll never understand."

"We'll get to the bottom of it," Officer Hughes says. "I'm going to go talk to that Vincent boy. He might have been here last night."

"I hope he wasn't," says Mr. Nibert. "He made it into high school this school year by working extra hard last summer. He's had problems, but is doing much better."

Officer Hughes shrugs. "Some juveniles can revert back to their devious ways. Witnesses said he was hanging around here with some kids last night and they were seen running from the building."

Mr. Nibert shakes his head. "Let's hope he is staying on track. He's a smart kid."

They walk along the hall to the fallen portraits. Nibert reaches down to pick one up.

Hughes distracts him. "Best to leave them until we finish investigating."

"All right," says Nibert. "I just hate seeing them on the floor like that. I want them up before we open the school again."

Hughes surveys the pictures lying about and then turns away from there to go to the stairway while Nibert remains to look over the pictures.

Hughes pauses at the top of the stairway. "I'll head over to that boy's house if you'll give me his address."

"I'm reluctant to," Nibert says, "but come down to the office."

I follow them down, sneaking beneath the handrail and watch them enter Nibert's office. I peek in and watch Nibert retrieve a folder. He writes an address on a piece of paper, and hands it to Hughes.

"Keep an open mind with Jackie," Nibert says.

Hughes looks like he's about to blurt out a *humph*. "I'm just going to ask him some questions; then I want to come back and meet," he says. "Will you be here?"

"All right, I'll meet you here. Say, eleven-thirty?"

Hughes leaves the office and Nibert resumes work at his desk.

This gives me some time: After what I've heard them say, I'm not going to allow an act by *whatever-it-is* ruin that boy. I will figure out the mystery behind it later, but now I wait while Hughes leaves and Nibert settles back into his office. Then I sneak back upstairs and go to the portraits. I have to be quiet as I take hold of Julia Gould's picture and lift it to the wall. It's difficult and it will take a long while to mount all of these back onto the wall. At least I got Miss Gould's back up where she belongs. I straighten her picture and look at the rest. No time to put more up now, but at least I can tip a couple up off the floor against the wall, face out. I go to Mary Service's picture and pull it up to lean against the wall. If I get a few more standing, it'll help.

* * *

Hughes knocks on the front door of Jackie's house on East Second Street and stands back. A young woman in a housecoat answers, her hair pinned up.

"Yes?" she says, tapping her hair back, looking embarrassed, trying not to sound nervous.

"Pardon me, ma'am," Hughes says. "Does Jackie Vincent live here and is your husband home?"

"Jackie is here and my husband was killed three months ago, serving in Germany," she says. "Is there any trouble, officer?"

Hughes removes his hat. "I'm sorry to hear of the death of your brave husband." He maintains his distance, twisting the mask around in his jacket pocket. "Well, was Jackie out for Halloween last night? There was to be no trick-or-treating this year."

"No, he didn't go trick-or-treating. He was with friends, but they stayed around here."

"May I talk to him?"

"Well, all right. I'll get him."

Hughes sits against the porch railing and waits.

A minute later, Mrs. Vincent emerges. "He's still in bed. There's no school now so he sleeps in, and I let him. Why do you need to see him?"

Hughes pulls out his notepad and pencil. "Just a couple of questions. Where was he last night between around 9:30 and midnight?"

She frowns for a moment. "He was here mostly. After 10:00, he was home. Why?"

"Did he go inside the grade school?"

"Of course not, it's locked."

"A witness saw him sneak in through a window a while back."

132

"Well, he didn't go in last night. What happened at the school?" she says, sitting on a porch chair.

"Vandalism," he says. "Somebody defaced the teacher portraits. I saw them this morning all over the hallway floor.

"That's terrible," she says.

"I'm going back over there to investigate more in a while. I'll be back here if I have more questions."

She shakes her head and goes back inside.

Hughes heads down the porch steps and walks west toward Mulberry school.

When he enters, he and Nibert go to the second floor and stroll to the portrait hall. They notice Miss Gould's portrait has returned to the wall and other portraits are leaning against the wall now.

"What happened here, Nibert?" Hughes asks in an accusing manner.

"I have no idea."

"You should know—did you arrange these to protect the boy?"

"No. I don't know what happened here. I've been in my office."

From behind the radiator, I think: And you never will know, gentlemen, but I will figure out what happened.

* * *

That evening, hours later when the building is empty, I stroll around the halls to engage my regular pacing-thinking and go past Maggie's door once more, then down to the portrait hall.

The portraits still clutter the floor and the ones I lifted to stand against the wall are back on the floor. Mary Service's picture is face down as is Miss Gould's.

Eric T. Reynolds

These events by whatever-it-is keep getting personal, and I won't stand for that. Sooner or later, I'll get whatever-it-is to show itself.

November 11, 1918

The first Armistice Day

"Isn't it wonderful!" said Rose, who just arrived at the Oxford amid an early gathering of activity on Main Street. Maggie and Mrs. Thrall greeted her.

George and Nancy Fielding entered. "The war is over!" George shouted. "People are assembling for a spur of the moment parade!"

Cheering spread among all of them; they went to the window to watch where people had formed a line of cars on North Main Street, excited drivers already honking their horns. More citizens joined the parade from side streets with various noise-making devices.

Mrs. Thrall went to the kitchen, brought a small basket of bread and toast, and offered it to Maggie, who thanked her.

"Shall we go?" said Maggie, taking the basket out to the porch. She and the others watched as the cars started rolling past, decorated with flags and dragging milk cans tied to the back bumpers making a clanking racket, the cars filled with people cheering along with more marchers who joined carrying flags, banging on buckets and tubs as the noise level surged.

Maggie, Rose, George and Nancy went down to the curb and joined a row of marchers. A marcher had an extra bucket within another and offered it to George who started banging his fist on it. Maggie jumped over next to Nancy; she and Nancy hit the bucket as well. A woman behind them had two flags and tapped Rose to offer her one. She took it and continued to contribute to the noise as they roared down Main Street. When they crossed Sixth Street, more revelers joined them, some with cow bells, tin pans, and anything that made noise to add to roar of horns and cheering. Maggie and others had to step around trails of detached milk cans, buckets, and other noise makers. When they reached the courthouse block, Maggie noticed rising smoke ahead to the south. A slight step to the side and the burning pile of boxes was visible, people adding to it as the fire roared higher. A band was assembling there.

At Third Street Jackie came from the side and ran up next to Maggie.

"Why, Jackie!" she shouted over the clamor, placing her hand on his shoulder.

"Wow!" he shouted, "I had to come to this! My pop was killed fighting for us."

"We're proud of him," shouted Maggie.

"Thank you." He pointed ahead. "Mom is up ahead somewhere." He went on, a spring in his step.

"One of your students?" Rose said.

"He was. He's in high school now."

Rose nodded. "I remember him. Glad he made it."

They continued south along Main, past stores whose proprietors stood on the sidewalks cheering the parade on as revelers walked along the Opera House Block, where people shouted from upper windows.

When Maggie and her friends reached the bonfire around River Street, they stopped and found an opening in the gathering semicircle of spectators. The band played patriotic songs just loud enough to hear over the cheering behind.

Doris stood in the semicircle across from them. She waved toward Maggie and friends. Rose started to return the wave, then looked behind them and noticed Abby there waving back at Doris.

"Hello, Abby," Rose said.

"Hello, Rose, Maggie, George, Nancy," Abby said. "What a day this is." She tapped Rose and Maggie on the shoulders. "Excuse me," she said, as she stepped back through the crowd to make her way around to Doris.

After a while, Doris and Abby headed east along River Street.

Most of the marchers and cars in the procession were heading back north now, carrying a steady din of cheering, honking, and other racket with them.

Maggie and friends went along Main Street and window shopped at a few stores. Maggie peered into Eureka Electric & Ice store.

"Look," she said, pointing to a mahogany finish Victrola console with a sign that read "Victrola the Eighteenth" with a small card that said "$300."

They looked for a moment more, then continued north.

Rose stopped in front of Frank H. Brooks. "I think they're having a sale soon," she said.

"And I need a winter suit," said Maggie, looking at the displays.

Ahead, portions of the parade split off to the west and east onto Second Street, taking some commotion with them.

As Maggie and friends continued north alongside the parade, a woman with Jackie broke from the marchers and ran over to Maggie. She grabbed Maggie's hand. "Miss Stilwell, remember me? Mrs. Vincent? I want to thank you for all you've done for Jackie! I'm sorry I haven't had a chance to meet with you all this time. With losing Jackie's father, everything's been challenging for us at home and I'm so glad Jackie's made it to high school."

Maggie shook Mrs. Vincent's hand. "Yes, of course. He's a fine boy. And smart. I'm happy he's moving along now."

"He really is, and he's looking forward to when school opens up again." Jackie tugged on her hand. "Oh, well it was great to run into you. We're going to go back out to the parade."

Maggie and Rose continued on. George and Nancy bid goodbye and rejoined the parade.

"Say, Rose," said Maggie, "I meant to tell you I got a letter from Ricky's cousin Clyde. He and Marie have invited us to spend Thanksgiving dinner with them in El Dorado."

"Yes, sounds lovely," said Rose.

November 28, 1918

Maggie

In the wee hours of the morning, Maggie rolled over and looked toward the mantle clock sitting on her dresser. She wouldn't normally be able to see it in the dark but for the swath of moonlight streaming in through the window, casting a brilliant spot onto the clock face. The clock displayed: Eight-thirty.

Clyde was going to be here at nine! She sat up and was about to rush to the bathroom until she realized she had let the clock wind down this time so she wouldn't have to listen to clunk-clunk-clunk-clunk during the night. Before she lay back down, she went to the window to look for the Moon. It wasn't where she would expect it to be with the moonlight spot on the clock, so she looked out and around for a window or something else that might be reflecting it, but couldn't find anything. Too tired to figure it out now, she got into bed and tried to get back to her dream, which she could do sometimes if she could relax, but they always ended up a little different from where she left off. She drifted into her usual floating realm of school, friends, and home. And the persona of a kind friend she struggled to meet. He usually came by to visit and something prevented her from getting to the living room to greet him. This time it was another persona who tried to woo her from the kind one. She went to another room in the dream where the kind persona sat smiling at her as she entered. She went

139

to the chair across from him, but something prevented her from sitting.

A slight knock stirred her to a half-conscious state and she opened an eye, and realized what it was. A mouse trap must have tripped outside her door. She rolled out of bed, cracked the door, and peeked into the hall where light from the bathroom down the way cast a feeble glow. The trap wasn't tripped and the bait was still there. She closed the door and went back to bed, stretched and lay back down.

No resuming a continuation dream this time after she drifted back to sleep. This one focused again on the struggle to reach the kind persona, and the rest of the night she spent periodically waking and looking around.

When glimmers of dawn emerged outside, she managed to doze for a while until sunlight spilled into her room and reflected off a hand mirror propped up on her desk. The reflected sunlight cast a spot onto the dresser, to the now-glinting card holder. She lay there for a moment, gazed at the silver object, and thought about Ricky for a while. What if the accident hadn't happened? Would they be spending Thanksgiving together?

Then she sighed and sat up.

As she went down the hall to the bathroom, she decided to wear her new wool suit that she had bought two weeks before at the Frank H. Brooks End of War Sale. It was good timing considering the recent cold snap and with the temperature in the thirties outside this morning.

When she was dressed and ready, she checked her hair, patted the card holder, smiled, and put it in her purse. Then she went down to have a light breakfast. From her seat at the table, she noticed a few flurries floating through the waning fall foliage.

"Here's the paper," Mrs. Thrall said, handing the *Wichita Eagle* to Maggie. "I'll have a copy of the *Herald* later, too."

Maggie opened to the weather section. Scanning down with her finger, she came to the Moon phases.

"I thought so," she said, finding that the Moon was a waning crescent during the night, far to the west and in the wrong place at that time to shine into her room. She abandoned the puzzle and went to the living room.

A little later, Rose arrived to join her for when Clyde came by to take them to El Dorado for Thanksgiving dinner at their home.

"Whew," Rose said. "I'm glad we were spared the snow Topeka got."

Maggie nodded. "Good thing. And I'm so glad Clyde and Marie asked me to invite you."

"It'll be nice. Thanksgiving will be more relaxed with John gone."

"It'll be hard for the Snyders after losing their son in last Friday's football game."

"That was so tragic, that poor young man."

"Reuben was one of my students. Very bright and well liked. It's so sad."

A horn outside interrupted them as a shiny new Pontiac pulled up. Clyde came up to the living room and the women donned their coats.

"Good morning, ladies," Clyde said. "The car's comfortable. The heater warmed it up well on the drive over."

"Let's go," said Maggie.

They climbed into the car and started on their way down Main Street, passing by Ricky's rooming house.

Maggie winked at it and smiled.

"Ricky and I spent a lot of Thanksgivings together since we were boys," Clyde said. "I can tell you some stories."

"I'll look forward to that," said Maggie.

Rose agreed.

After a moment, they reached River Street which led west to the highway. They drove along it and approached some of the higher Flint Hills with twin mounds ahead. To the northeast, a distinctive hill rose above the landscape.

"Sugar Loaf," said Rose, pointing to it.

"Ricky worked on an oil rig up past there," Clyde said.

Maggie gazed at the rolling hills beneath the gray sky. Her mind began to wander and she closed her eyes.

Had Ricky remained on that job, he'd probably still be alive. On the other hand, had he never taken the oil rig job, he wouldn't have left it to take the construction job and he might not have moved to Eureka. But me not ever knowing him is not worth him dying. That's not a hard one to figure out.

She drifted to sleep, the fitful night catching up to her, but the nap only lasting a few minutes. They were ascending around the north side of the smaller twin mound. Gazing out to the right rewarded her with a view of occasional yellow-leafed cottonwoods and tallgrass that covered the rolling hills rimmed by boulders. She closed her eyes again and slept longer this time.

* * *

When she awoke, they were driving along a tree-lined neighborhood street in El Dorado. Clyde and Marie's large foursquare house had fresh piles of newly-raked leaves beneath tall oaks, still holding some orange leaves. They pulled into the drive and Clyde got out first. He opened the back-seat door and offered his hand to assist both women onto the running board. Maggie stepped from it onto the driveway and pulled her coat tightly against the chill.

Marie met them at the door and showed them into the spacious living room, took their coats, and invited them to sit on the chairs next to the fireplace, placing a plate of crackers and cheese and pot of tea with cups on the coffee table near them.

Clyde sat on a chair across from them. "I hope you enjoyed the ride over."

Rose nodded approval. "Yes. Maggie had a nice nap. On my shoulder, no less."

"Didn't sleep well last night," said Maggie.

"I'm sorry to hear that," Clyde said. "While we wait, I have a couple of stories to tell."

Maggie leaned forward. "Yes?"

"Well," started Clyde, "Ricky was several years younger than I was and my aunt and uncle who are gone now, used to bring him over from Eureka to visit up till he was nine and I was twelve. He was a skinny kid, but very active. Now, there was a bully in the neighborhood named Jim Holly who picked on anyone smaller than he was. Ricky and I were playing catch at the park when Holly appeared and went over to a little neighborhood kid demanding money for playing in "his" park. The boy refused and Holly started to grab him. The kid ran and Holly chased him. Ricky ran after them. The kid rushed toward the street, so scared he was about to run out in front of a car. Ricky ran as fast as he could, reaching the street first and jumped out toward the middle of the street. The car lurched away, missing both of them.

"When we were older after his family moved over here, he used to like to go to the courthouse on Central Avenue. He went on and on about the architecture. 'It's Romanesque architecture,' he'd say, 'designed by George P. Washburn & Sons.' It was built about ten years ago, 1908.' He also talked about the French Renaissance architecture of your Greenwood County Courthouse. We figured he'd want to study architecture someday and he said he wanted to visit every county courthouse in Kansas."

"I wish I could have talked to him about these things," said Maggie. "It sounds fascinating and it seems he was so knowledgeable." She sighed. "So many good things missed."

Marie and her mother entered and announced dinner was ready.

* * *

After dinner, Clyde invited Maggie and Rose into his paneled study and asked them to sit.

Opening a desk drawer, he retrieved an envelope. "I don't know if Ricky would have wanted this read aloud, but here it is."

Dear Clyde,

I'm getting settled in here in Eureka. People seem friendly enough and there's a young lady in the rooming home near me who looks smart and appears friendly. I made a clumsy fool of myself in the post office in front of her. She just laughed and helped me gather my letters off the floor. I took an instant liking toward her. I'd like to talk to her if I could get up the nerve. You know how I am ever since junior high, I would never talk to girls because I didn't think I was good enough and other fellows did and I didn't want to compete with them. This woman is so nice. She seems unattached, not courting anyone. She walked by my rooming house yesterday and we caught each other's eye. She smiled and I smiled back. Well, that did it. I asked one of the men in my rooming home about her. He confirmed her name is Maggie and she teaches eighth grade. I'll write again and let you know how things are going here, including Maggie if I ever talk to her.

Yours,

Ricky

"Thank you, Clyde," said Maggie. "I remember that day when I first saw him. I had similar feelings as he. I've wondered if I should have approached him. Do you think that would have been too forward?"

Clyde shook his head. "No."

"No," echoed Rose.

"I agree. I've always dismissed the idea of being too forward," said Maggie. "Had I approached him more, we might have had a different outcome."

"How are you doing day to day, Maggie?" Clyde asked.

"School work keeps me busy, even with school being closed these past few weeks."

"I read that Eureka will reopen schools on Monday," he said.

"Indeed," Maggie said. "I miss my students and am eager to get back on schedule."

November 29, 1918

Ricky

It's quiet, of course this late. I go to the hall of portraits
to check on the pictures. They were placed nicely on the
walls in their original positions a couple of days ago.
Principal Nibert got his wish to have the portraits back
up before school reopens this Monday. I'm glad of that.
I'm also glad that Maggie will be back, which might be a
bit self-centered of me. But then, I don't know how not
to be in this state of being since I can't relate directly with
people, and all I have is my limited one-sided
communication. I imagine Maggie will be happy to return
and get things back to normal. I hope she has time to talk
to me again. Until then, I'll pace around the rest of the
building. Miss Gould looks as nice as usual and Miss
Service looks as if saying, "Don't you dare mess with our
portraits again." Whatever-it-is best heed the warning and
stay away or there'll be consequences. I'll make sure of
that.

I go along the wide hallway as if I'm an inspector
checking to verify satisfactory conditions for the
students' return in three days. I can never resist stopping
at Maggie's classroom door when I'm in this hall. I press
my face through her door and everything's fine; her
classroom looks like she hasn't been in since I last peeked
a couple of weeks ago. I head down to the gym and look
for the side horse. It's nowhere to be found. I mosey
around to one of the basketball goals and am tempted to

146

jump and bat the net to free it up. I turn back the other direction and the side horse is right in front of me now. I ignore it, go around it, and look around the gym more. All seems in order except waving stage curtains. I go over to the stage and ascend onto it. The curtains settle down, and I hear a thump in the hall outside the gym. I go there and hear something in the southeast stairway. I find nothing at the landing area and follow another thump down to the basement, to the end of the short hall past the boiler room. I push my face through the door. Everything's in order.

Another thump. Something upstairs. I'm going upstairs anyway so I head back to the stairway, go up to the main floor landing, and pause. All quiet. I go on up to the second-floor landing where I enter the long hallway. It's quiet and dark except for a soft knocking down by the portraits at the far end of the hall. I go that way, following the bumps and knocks: past the library, past the restrooms, toward the main hallway and the portraits. When I reach them, I scan around to check them and they're all still fine.

I want to walk by Maggie's room again so I head there, and on the way, I brush my hand along the lockers and reach her classroom. I miss seeing her, but I have to bide my time until she returns. Three days is a short time in the overall scheme of things, so I should be able to manage the wait.

I continue pacing. I head back toward the main hallway to the shadowy end and the portraits. I pass the stairs and the current affairs class on the way. I walk toward the portraits and pause just before I reach them to listen. I hear a faint sound like a squeaky hinge oscillating, barely there. I focus on the source. It's in the direction of Miss Gould's portrait. I go to it. It's swinging on the wall. I reach to steady it, but something blocks my hand. The portrait starts to nudge itself upward. I reach to take hold of it, but something blocks me again. The portrait inches up off the hanger and falls to the floor before I can catch it.

I reach down to pick it up. It's heavier than normal. I try to heave it up the best I can. I'm losing my hold on it. Something is trying to force it from my grip. I hang onto it before it falls to the floor, but it slips away. Now it lays there, so I bend down to it, but something blocks me. The portrait slides a couple of feet away from me. I scramble toward it. Something invisible pushes me over. I start flailing out and my hands land on it. Something invisible lands on my jaw. I punch out toward it and bash something.

A luminescent figure the shape of a man appears on the floor next to me. It stands; I stand and face it.

"What are you doing!" I shout.

He answers with a jab, just missing my chin. I return my own jab. He throws himself into me and we crash to the floor. I grab and pull him around; we roll over along the floor. He grabs Miss Gould's picture and throws it against a wall.

"That's personal!" I blurt out. I stand, pull him up, and belt him in the jaw.

He steps back.

"Do I have your attention now?" he says.

"Who are you?" I say.

"Your rival," he says.

"I mean, what's your name?"

"You mean: what *was* my name?"

"Right. Who were you?"

"I was Gerald Cline."

"I didn't know you."

"No, I was born fifteen years before you."

"When did you die?"

"November 1903," he says.

"How?"

"A month before then, I worked on the crew that installed the gasoline engine that ran the new heating system in Eastside School."

"And you died in an accident there?" I ask.

"No. I had the accident in October, but I didn't die then. We were working on the engine, and my hand got caught in the ventilation fan, The shock almost killed me, but didn't. I lost two fingers. After a week or so, I came down with blood poisoning and died in early November."

"Anything you want to know about me?" I ask. "I was Ricky Austin."

"Why are you here?" Gerald asks.

"I died in a fall here while we were building this school," I say.

"You're the fool who plunged from the ceiling because you got scared."

I want to hit him again. "I couldn't help it. I froze, then slipped. Why are you trying to get me angry?"

"You need to stop interfering here, stop helping, stop intervening in things." Gerald says.

"I'm not going to stop. You're interfering. Are you behind some of the pranks and vandalism? Did you make the picture fall in Maggie's class when her friend walked in? Did you push Maggie's card holder into the waste basket so Mr. Martin would throw it out?"

"I had nothing to do with the picture falling in Maggie's room, but I did push the card holder."

"You had no right to do that with the card holder. That's precious to her."

"I insist you stop interfering," Gerald says.

"You stop," I say. "Did you spell out that message on the kids' Ouija Board?"

"What do you think?" he says.

Eric T. Reynolds

"I think you did," I say. "What about the women who came in on Halloween? What did you do to scare them?"

"I won't tolerate more invasion of my domain," he says.

"They paid for this building. They have every right to be here, no matter the reason."

"They don't. I need my solitary place," he says.

"Am I also invading your domain?" I ask.

"Yes."

"Nerts! Where am I supposed to go?"

"You can confine yourself to a room, hall, or what have you," Gerald says.

"So you can have the whole place for your solitude?" I say. "What is your claim to this place?"

"I died from working in Eastside School that occupied this location," he says.

"How does that overrule my claim?" I ask.

"I was first." He walks away.

"This conversation isn't over," I say.

November 30, 1918

Maggie, et al

About mid-afternoon, Maggie, Rose, and Annie walked into the main hallway, their loud footsteps bouncing off walls near and far.

"Listen to us," said Annie. "Our heels are loud enough to wake the dead." She stopped and put her hand to her mouth. "Oh—I'm so sorry, you two!"

Maggie didn't answer nor did Rose, and Annie was quiet for a while.

"It's all right, Annie. I'm all for waking the dead," Maggie finally said as they went up to the second floor toward Maggie's classroom. George's door was open and Annie went over to it.

"Mr. Fielding is here," she said.

They joined her, and George met them there. "Hello, ladies. Just getting ready for Monday."

Annie glanced at the chalkboard which was full of math problems and illustrations. "Are you going to welcome your students back with that?" Annie said. "I hope they don't turn around and walk out."

"Math is fun," he said. "What matters is how it's taught." He went back to the board, erased a problem, and replaced it with another. "Thank you, Miss Marsh, I meant to include this one instead."

"Way to go, Annie," said Maggie, smiling. "That one's even harder."

George brushed the chalk dust from his hands and returned to his work as they left to cross over to Maggie's room.

Maggie went to her chalkboard and wrote "Welcome back" in big letters. Below that: "Remember to wash your hands before and after eating and after using the restroom."

"The students will be returning to school without Reuben," she said. "It'll be hard for them. He was well liked. And an excellent student, not to mention being a handsome young man." She went to look out the window and dabbed her eyes with a handkerchief, then held her hand over the radiator.

Rose stepped over to put a hand on Maggie's shoulder. "I'm sorry, Maggie," she said.

Maggie smiled at her. "Thank you, Rose."

Annie came over to join them and said, "Reuben used to hurry into the library before football practice to check out a book and then run over to the high school for practice."

"I remember that," said Maggie. She waved her hand over the radiator again.

"Is it warm?" asked Annie.

"It's warm. Mr. Martin's got the boiler working well, in time for winter." She stepped to the row of desks along there. The afternoon sun flooded its brilliance onto the desks.

"What is it, Maggie?" asked Rose.

"I wonder if you both could help me move this row of desks over out of the sun."

"Of course we can," replied Rose.

"But not too far or they'll be too close to the next row," said Maggie.

Annie smiled. "We won't want the boys and girls sitting too close to each other."

They went to the row of desks. "Thank you," said Maggie. "These desks are heavy with those iron legs. Mr. Martin's got the floor nice and shiny so let's be careful not to scoot them across. I thought about asking him to move the desks, but he's got a lot to do."

After the three of them lugged the desks over, Maggie went to straighten pictures on the south wall and went to the calendar there to mark some dates for upcoming events.

The American flag hung flat on the north wall above the chalkboard. She stood on tiptoes and ran her hand across the fabric to flatten the wrinkles. Then she took the framed picture of author Margaret Hill McCarter from her desk to the east wall and placed it on the hanger that Mr. Martin had put there for her.

* * *

Later, when Maggie finished her tasks and had her room how she wanted it, and after the others left, she locked up, took the card holder from her purse, and went to the location of Ricky's accident. For a while, she stood still and allowed the silence to permeate her senses. After a few minutes, she sighed.

"Ricky," she said. "I thought about this moment for some time and am not sure where to start, because things have happened since I last spoke to you. We lost one of our eighth-graders. Reuben Snyder was playing in a football game against Burlington. He was only fourteen and was the youngest player on either team. His parents are devastated and many of us are in shock. As I did with you, I wonder what would have been in his future. What would he have been as an adult? Would he marry? Have children? We'll never know.

"Six of his classmates served as pall bearers at his funeral last Sunday afternoon. It was held at his family's home. The casket was covered high in beautiful flowers. I'm proud of his friends for their dignified service to their friend that day. When the rest of Reuben's classmates return on Monday, they'll need help coping with this tragedy. I can tell it already helps to talk to you. You're like a shoulder I can lean on. You probably didn't know him, but he was a delightful young man.

"Since we last talked, it was comforting that my attention was diverted when I learned more about you from a letter your cousin read to Rose and me. Where did you ever get the idea to run out in front of a car to save a little kid? Oh my, what quick thinking that was. Your cousin, Clyde thought of you as his little brother. He and Marie invited Rose and me over to their home for Thanksgiving, and he told us that story and about your fascination with architecture and the big plans you had. I knew that, of course. When Clyde mentioned your plan to visit every courthouse in Kansas, I had more 'what would have been' thoughts. And later, hee-hee, I thought of you going on a crime spree in every county in the state.

"Before you left us, I imagined us together, and what kind of home would have we. I didn't expect it would be anything large, a cute little place, maybe a smaller bungalow with a couple of bedrooms. In fact, I was thinking about that on my way to the high school quite possibly when you fell.

"Well, the war ended on November 11th, and we had a huge celebration all over town. No planning, a spur of the moment parade, up and down Main Street full of revelers and noise, noise, noise and a bonfire on South Main.

"Now, something that's puzzling me is the strange things going on here in the school. The falling portraits and such. I wish I knew why that's happening, although I have to admit I was amused at hearing about Doris's experience. But that's unkind of me to take pleasure in that. The incidents are troublesome, because I don't want

154

anything to be damaged or worse yet, someone get hurt. I'm sorry to bring this up. I'm not blaming you. They could be natural phenomena, but I don't know what could cause such things besides vandals...except these are happening when no one's around, it seems.

"Well, I'll drop the subject. That's not what I wanted to talk about after being away for so long.

"After poor Reuben's burial service, I walked around the cemetery and visited your grave. Clyde and Marie arranged for you to have a nice headstone. It's not installed yet, but I plan to visit it after it is. I have to say, I feel more connected to you here than I did out there, but then, I'm in the school building often, so it's convenient to talk here. When classes resume, I'll be back. I guess I will figure out these strange things going on soon enough."

"I'm looking forward to Monday, Ricky. Good-bye for now."

She gathered her coat together as she headed for the front doors.

December 2, 1918

Maggie

Maggie arrived the following Monday before the expected hubbub of the school reopening, and some of the other teachers were already in their rooms preparing for the return of eager students. When Maggie was opening her classroom door, George Fielding came over.

"Hello again," he said. "I'm glad I got ready over the weekend. It's hard to maintain continuity in math with a long absence. How about you?"

"I'm ready and have been looking forward to getting back," she said. "I miss my students."

He nodded. "If you're all settled in then I'll go attend to my room. It sounds like some students are arriving."

She went into her classroom and double checked everything. A fresh apple sat on her desk with a note.

On behalf of Reuben's family, we appreciated you as his teacher, as did Reuben.

—Mr. and Mrs. Snyder

Maggie kept her composure and paced around her room trying to be strong for Reuben's classmates. His empty desk in the second row on the right side of the room caught her eye.

"It'll be especially hard for his neighbors there," she said softly. "And his many friends."

The students started to enter, and after they took their seats, Maggie got started.

"Hello, everyone, welcome back. It's been difficult for us. I was going to pick up where we left off, but I've decided not to." She went to the board and found a clear area to write the title of a story from the book *Classics for the Kansas Schools, Eighth Grade*. She decided at this time against assigning the story that dealt with death, that she had chosen before the closing. They could read it later.

She gave them time to read today's story in class and during the quiet, she thought again about Ricky like a good friend whose imaginary shoulder she could lean on during this time of loss, a kind of uplifting feeling within her. When the class period drew to a close, the bell rang and her students got up and left. She went out to the hall to stretch her legs and walked around for a bit. Her next class didn't meet for another hour, so she strolled around to the portraits area. All of them were well positioned. As she gazed around at them, something caught her eye beneath Mary Service's portrait, a slight smudge on the wall under it, rather unsightly if one looked closely, but hopefully not that noticeable. She ignored it and went back toward her room, stopping to stand next to the wall between the radiator and her classroom door for a bit. She felt an internal warmth here, not just from the radiator; she thought about Ricky now and how she couldn't wait to talk to him again. This seemed like a pleasant place to be until it was time to return to class so she remained until then.

Jackie approached her. "Hi, Miss Stilwell," he said.

"Well, hello, Jackie," she said smiling. "How is high school Freshman year treating you?"

"I got an A on my last theme paper in English," he said.

"That's excellent," she said. "I'm so proud of you! What brings you by?"

"Miss Fuller sent me to pick up something from Mr. Fielding. I know Reuben was in your class. We miss him. He was a swell guy. How are you and the kids here doing?"

"It's hard for everyone. We teachers are being as compassionate as we can as the kids adjust back into school with him gone. Most of them were looking forward to coming back; then Reuben's tragedy struck."

"A lot of us at the high school are taking it pretty hard, too," he said. "For an eighth-grader, he was some football player and an excellent athlete. The seniors and juniors all liked him."

Maggie patted his shoulder and he headed to George's room while she went to the restroom before class.

December 2, 1918

Ricky

That same day, I've been in my hiding place for a while behind the second-floor hallway radiator as the students exit their classrooms, some congregating and getting into their lockers across from me. Maggie has arrived from the portraits area down the hall and stands against the wall not far from me. It's good to see her.

But Gerald is within shouting distance and now it's time for me to have it out with him; he is down by the portraits.

I ease my head up from the radiator.

"Geraaaaald!" I yell as loud as I can to him with my non-voice. I know he can hear me while the students and Maggie can't. "Come out, you stowaway!"

There he is, down against the wall next to Mary Service's portrait.

"Stowaway, nothing!" he yells back.

"I have something to say to you!" I shout.

"Then come down here and say it!"

"No! You come here after the students clear out!" I shout.

"You scaredy cat!" he yells.

After the last few students leave the hallways for their classrooms, Gerald's smudge slides around the wall's edge and hugs the floor as it passes by the front stairway, slithers toward me, then rears up in front of the radiator.

"Get behind here, stupid, so no one sees you," I say. He drops and slides beneath the radiator then stands behind the other end from me.

"What do you want, loser?" he says.

"You complain about me interfering, but it's you who interferes!" I say.

"Interferes in what!" he says.

"Maggie and me. You've got her wondering if I'm responsible for the shenanigans going on."

"You are!"

I'm tempted to lunge at him. "I would never do that!"

"Indirectly, you are responsible."

"How?"

"By trespassing in my domain, my solitude, so I have to scare people to make them and you want to leave," he says.

"Ridiculous. We settled that."

"We didn't," he says. "Stop helping people here."

"What's wrong with helping?" I ask.

"You're manipulating people's actions so they avoid getting hurt. But if bad things happen, people will leave," he says.

"I'm manipulating how?"

"Making the librarian trip over a marble," he says.

"That loose bulletin board could have really hurt her," I say. "And I didn't like how Miss Owens treated her students, so I interfered."

"And saving Maggie's card holder," he says.

"That was personal!"

"All right, I misjudged on that one," he says, "but you can't interfere with the natural course of events."

"Do I understand only you can do that?"

"Mine are targeted toward you."

"Again, you make no sense."

"Then get a break from me. Go out exploring."

"How? I can't go outside."

"Have you tried?" he asks.

"No, because I'll be seen."

"You can figure out how to evade that like I have."

"I doubt it."

"Don't you want to explore the world out there?" he says.

"How do you do it?" I ask.

"It's natural for me. The grounds here were part of Eastside School."

"Did you happen upon that ability right away?"

"Soon after," he says, "like I said, it's natural for me. There's a lot outside. You should go out."

"Before my accident," I say, "I used to hear about sightings of apparitions. Was that you?"

"How long ago?"

"It's been a while."

"Where?"

"West of town in some woods along a country road."

"I've refined my stealth abilities since then."

"I don't see how I can do that," I say.

"Go take a look at Maggie outside of a school setting."

"No."

"Aren't you curious about her?"

"She tells me a lot when she comes in," I say. "I look forward to that."

"Wouldn't you like to see her more often?" he asks.

"Of course I would."

"Then try," he says. "I've seen Maggie out there, and I've watched her sleep."

"You haven't!"

"She looks nice lying there with her eyes closed," he says. "Probably dreaming of you. Wouldn't you like to see that?"

"No," I say.

"Come on, didn't you used to have urges for her?" he says.

"Naturally I did, but I wanted to meet her and get to know her," I say. "I never even got to do that."

"She's lovely in a way," he says, "not the prettiest girl around."

"She's the most beautiful woman in Eureka," I say.

"Then go out and observe her," he says.

"It's natural for you to go out, not me," I say. "Why are you so concerned about your so-called domain here if you can go out any time?"

"This is my home. I don't want to share it. I already have to share it with the crowds during school."

"Then find a place to go when school's in session," I say.

He grumbles. "I'll bide my time—and you must as well."

"For what?"

"I'll let you know that when I know you're ready," he says.

December 21, 1918

Maggie

Maggie, Rose, and Annie emerged from the Princess Theatre auditorium into the lobby after the Saturday afternoon showing of *The Eyes of the Mummy*.

Maggie excused herself to the restroom and went to the far stall. A small group of girls entered, talking about the movie. Maggie couldn't see them and guessed three of them had entered together. She didn't recognize their voices; they sounded like they were in high school.

"So creepy," one girl said.

"I got goosebumps every time the mummy showed," said a second. "At least I only screamed once."

"You screamed every time," a third said, giggling. "And then, back in England, Ma's haunted by that Egyptian priest."

"If I had known before," one said, "I might not have let you all talk me into coming to this movie."

Now Maggie recognized her former student, Martha.

"I can tell you, I won't be going in dark places alone," said a second.

"Like Mulberry," the third said. "Did you hear what happened to those two ladies at Mulberry?"

"My mother knows one of them," Martha said.

"Scared by the ghost of that guy who died during construction," the second said. "Miss Stilwell still mourns him."

"Weird," the third said. "I heard she talks to him."

"And she's still teaching?" the second said.

"She's a good teacher," Martha said.

"Yes she is," the second said, "but I heard she keeps a crystal ball in her desk and tells students' fortunes."

"Say," the third said in a whisper that Maggie could just hear, "want to have some fun?"

"When?" the second asked.

"This afternoon," the third said.

"Maybe before four, so the janitor is still there and we can sneak in," the second said.

"Shall we meet there in about an hour?"

"I don't know," Martha said. "I don't like sneaking about."

"How are we getting in her room?" the second asked.

The third said, "Jackie Vincent knows how to get in places and I heard he likes me. He'll help us if I promise him a kiss."

"Ewww," the second said.

"I think he's kind of cute," the third said.

They snickered and Maggie waited until she was sure they had left and she went to the sink.

Rose and Annie came in.

"I just heard some high school girls in here planning to sneak into Mulberry," said Maggie. "I need to get up there before they do."

"What are they going to do?" asked Annie.

"I don't know," said Maggie, "but I think they're going to sneak in while Mr. Martin is still there. And— one of them is going to try to coerce Jackie into helping them."

They went out to the lobby and headed for the exit out to a mild December cool afternoon where sunny skies and temperature in the low 50s greeted them.

"I just came up with an idea of my own," said Maggie.

"Oh, what?" said Rose.

"I'll tell you if it works."

Maggie, Rose, and Annie walked along the sidewalk for a ways until Maggie went east on Third Street. Most of the trees were barren of leaves now. She wanted to check near Jackie's house and watched for any appearance of the girls to keep her distance if she saw them going toward his house. She reached Greenwood Street and thought she heard their voices to the south a block away on Second Street. As she suspected, two of the girls were headed straight for Jackie's house.

So Jackie would be put to a test today, she thought. How dare they! But then, she shouldn't be surprised at them. And Jackie could take care of himself. She would like to wait to see how that went, but she needed to head over to Mulberry School.

When she reached the school, it appeared Mr. Martin was still there, perhaps in the basement, so she hurried up into her room and opened a window a few inches. On the chalkboard, she wrote in medium-sized block letters:

MARTHA, BE CAREFUL WHEN YOU
CHOOSE YOUR FRIENDS
FOR THEY MIGHT STEER YOU WRONG
AND YOU'LL END UP LIKE THEM.

Maggie knew Martha probably wouldn't come in with the other girls, but maybe her friends would take a message from this. She took an eraser and lightly patted the words to blur them just a little, then took out two sheets of paper from her desk and wrote on both, also in block letters:

MARTHA, THEY WON'T WANT TO KNOW
WHAT AWAITS THEM.
and
DO YOU WANT THAT FOR YOURSELF?

She placed the first note in her middle desk drawer and the other note in the side drawer, both facing up, and left the drawers open. After removing her grade book, she went and listened out the window. She thought she heard girls' voices outside, so she took her gradebook and went into the hall, leaving her door unlocked. A distant door opening startled her. She took off her shoes and crept over to the nearby north stairway. Soft walking sounds and a peep from a girl revealed where they came in. They were on the main floor north hall heading toward these stairs.

Maggie tiptoed east down the side hall to the northeast stairway landing at the end and peeked down to make sure the girls didn't go over that way to sneak up here. New soft walking sounds came from the north stairway back near her classroom. Maggie ducked behind a wall to peer down the hall. Two girls stood outside her classroom. Maggie was curious to know what they planned, but she was thrilled to see Jackie wasn't with them. She heard their voices when they went into her classroom, laughing followed by more frantic chatter. Maggie went downstairs to the first-floor landing and almost shrieked when she saw Mr. Martin standing there.

"Everything all right, Miss Stilwell?" he asked.

"Yes, but some high school girls just sneaked into my classroom."

"I know," he said. "I saw them and I was going to confront them." He cupped his ear. "I'd better go. It sounds like they're running down the stairs in a panic over there."

"Go outside and head them off," suggested Maggie.

"Right," he said, dashing out the door.

Maggie went to watch the playground area. The girls ran up to Mr. Martin and hugged him. Maggie heard cries of relief and Mr. Martin gently shoved them away, sent them on their way, and they ran from sight.

"Well," he said when he returned, "something scared them." He produced two wadded pieces of paper. "One of them had these. I hope nothing important."

Maggie took one, unfolded it and laughed. "I planted these notes for them to find."

"Scared them," he said.

"I'm glad. They were going to be rummaging around in my desk, so I left it open after I found out what they were up to. And, oh, I messed up that nice clean chalkboard."

"I'll re-clean it for you."

"I'm sorry," said Maggie, "I didn't mean…"

"It's no problem," he insisted.

They went up to the second floor to her classroom.

"Well then," he said, staring at the board. "I'm glad I ran into you or I would have run away screaming after seeing this, too."

Maggie laughed. "Well, but you know better."

"I'm not so sure," he said.

* * *

On her way out when she was sure the main floor hallway was empty, she went to the accident scene.

"Hi, Ricky. I'm worried you'll get blamed for the girls' encounter. I'm sorry about that. When I heard them talking in the restroom down at the Princess Theatre, I couldn't resist setting up a scare for them. I was so glad Jackie wasn't with them. I don't like it when I find out that someone else is talking about me keeping your memory alive, and now by high school kids. I had hoped, perhaps naïvely, it would remain only with the adults around town."

Maggie clenched her fists and groaned.

"I don't care! I'm talking to you when I can and keeping your memory alive—whatever people say!"

Her shout echo bounced like always, these taking longer to subside. Now, rapid footsteps sounded down the side hall, and Mr. Martin came around the corner.

"Miss Stilwell! What's wrong?"

"It's fine," she said. "Just releasing some frustration. The acoustics are just right in here for that," she said, smiling a little.

"I'm sorry that you're having frustration," he said, his expression showing empathy.

She shrugged. "I shouldn't pay attention to those things."

"What things?"

"Things people say about my devotion to the memory of that poor man," she said. Then she pointed up. "Of Ricky Austin who fell from up there. Some of the criticism is harsh."

"I'm sorry they do those things, but not everyone is of those opinions."

"You're sure?"

He touched her wrists in his rough hands. "You are a special lady loved and respected by people in this town. Many people talk about you being an excellent and knowledgeable teacher, beloved by her students. I certainly understand your anguish and I'm sure others do, too. But I want you to take comfort in the fact that you can rise above the naysayers. Why, if Ricky would have known of your efforts after his leaving, he'd surely have been pleased."

"Mr. Martin, thank you."

"All right, then," he said. "I'm going to finish down in the boiler room and head on. Please lock up when you leave. See you on the 30th if not before." He went to the side hallway and his footsteps faded.

"Ricky," she said. "I'm happy to know those things, and I do hope you would have been pleased. I believe I'll go now and get to reading a book I bought the other day. I think Monday, the 30th when school re-opens again will be hectic and I will try to come in and talk before then."

She took the card holder out, brought it to her lips, and left.

December 23, 1918

Maggie

Mid-morning, in the Oxford's living room, Maggie sat by the fireplace, warmed by the roaring fire. She put her book down for a moment and gazed over out the front bay windows at the snow that was falling at a rapid rate, already accumulating several inches onto Main Street. It was a far cry from the day before when she enjoyed an unusually warm seventy-degree day. Once this storm finished, she didn't think she'd get out until the sidewalks were cleared and so she didn't know when she could get into school to talk to Ricky. She pulled the throw blanket around her and enjoyed the cozy warmth as she watched the growing flakes drift down.

Another Oxford resident joined her, taking a seat on the bay window sofa. Norma Marshall was older, a widow and Maggie saw her occasionally, although not as much as she would have liked, but she realized that was her own fault. Maggie should have asked her to join her here more often. As someone who was decades older than Maggie, Norma was a direct link to history: the stories she could tell.

Shoveling outside interrupted Maggie's thoughts. Mr. MacGregor, Mrs. Thrall's handyman, was busy clearing the Oxford's front sidewalk.

"That's something I don't miss." Norma said. "I had to take care of it and other chores at our house after Abe passcd away."

"Oh?" asked Maggie. "I'm sorry, when did you lose your husband?"

"Five years ago in an automobile accident over by Yates Center. He was a kind man and ornery to boot."

Maggie leaned forward.

"Well, yes," Norma continued. "Abe was on the original construction crew that built Eastside School in 1873. I was around your age then. He was three years older than I was and quite the practical joker. We were courting then, and as a young lady, I wasn't privy to all his shenanigans, but one day…

* 1873 *

Norma walked along the recently maintained gravel and dirt road toward the building site. The stone schoolhouse was nearly complete, the only building in that area of Mulberry Street. Several men tended to their horses at a hitching post along the street next to a water trough. A couple of wagons loaded with building materials sat on the far side of the building.

She saw men gathered beneath a tree near a water well pump. Abe was there chattering as usual. Norma straightened her hat and flipped her skirt around and brushed it flat, making sure it hadn't ridden up to her ankles, what with all those men there.

She timed it right; the men were on their lunch break. She carried a lunch bucket of something special to Abe, her succotash recipe, his favorite of her dishes. The men stood when she reached them, those wearing hats tipped them. Abe went to her.

"Thank you for bringing the lovely lady to entertain us," Brock Howard said.

Norma looked embarrassed. Abe took Norma's hand walked with her to the well.

"Just a moment, darling," he said. "I know it's here." He bent down and fiddled with the spout.

"Come on over, Howard," he said, "bring your cup and I'll pump some water for you."

Brock joined Abe and Norma at the well, placing his cup under the spout.

"Mighty friendly of you, Abe," he said. "And nothing personal in my comment, miss," he said to Norma.

She nodded, and Abe grabbed the handle and started pumping water into the cup. "Drink it real quick, Brock, while it's nice and cold," he said.

Abe stopped pumping the handle.

Brock brought the cup to his lips. "Ahhh!" he shouted. He dumped the water and jumped back from the wiggling baby ringneck snake his cup had held, then he threw his cup down. "I'll get you, Marshall!"

Norma went to cradle the little snake in her cupped hands and let it go on the other side of the tree. "There you go, poor little fellow," she said.

Abe was laughing so hard he lay in the grass on his back kicking like a baby.

* * *

Maggie also had a good laugh.

"Well," Norma said to Maggie, "Abe was so impressed with how I handled that snake, he proposed that evening. We married two months later."

"He sounds like quite a fellow," Maggie said.

"He was. I was lucky to have him. I wish he hadn't left so soon. You know? I still talk to him almost every day. One time, I was walking along Main Street, stopped at the railroad tracks, and just as I was thinking, 'I miss your practical jokes', a train slowed there to stop at the depot and right when the engine passed me, the whistle blew, scaring me half to death, and a puff of steam blew my dress up to my calves! After the train went on, I started laughing and shouted, 'Go on, Abe! You old rascal!'. The train blew its whistle and chugged away."

"That's amazing," said Maggie.

"It lifted my spirits that day," Norma said, and then reached to take Maggie's hand. "It was so sad about that young man who died during the construction of the new school. At least Abe had a good long life. I know that Austin young man was a friend of yours and I know you get criticized for still being sad about his accident."

"You've heard?"

"Oh yes. And let me tell you: don't you let it bother you. It's no one's business but yours. I admire you for not letting him go—whatever they say, it lets the town not forget him."

"Thank you, Norma. You're most kind."

"All right. You keep at it, young lady, you're to be commended."

"I'll keep remembering that," Maggie said.

Another resident, Hazel, a middle-aged woman who lived down and across the hall from Maggie entered the living room.

"Hello, everyone," she said. "If you're like me, any plans for going out today are dashed."

"It's disappointing, isn't it?" said Maggie. "Snowed in, but I guess that gives us all a chance to socialize."

"Then may I join you ladies?" Hazel asked, sitting on the sofa next to Norma.

"Of course," Maggie and Norma replied in unison.

"Thank you." Hazel took out a box of cards and put it onto the coffee table.

Mrs. Thrall came in from the kitchen with a plate of crackers and set it on the table to the side. "I should like to join you, too" she said.

The rest welcomed her and she scooted one of the fireplace chairs over to the coffee table. "Let's move you over, too, Maggie," she said.

"Do you all know how to play Logomachy," Hazel said, tapping the deck.

"I do," Maggie said. "But how about a quick review."

"Yes," Hazel said, putting her hand on the card deck. "First, we shuffle the deck and deal them out. Each card has a letter on it. We go around and place our cards on the table to spell words. If your card adds to the spelling of a word, you score."

"That sounds fun," Mrs. Thrall said.

"We played this when Abe was alive," Norma said with a chuckle. "He used to spell out insults to other players, the old coot."

They played for a couple of hours. Norma ended her last turn completing the word "laugh." Maggie ended her last turn completing the word "again."

December 25, 1918

Ricky

Mid-morning, Christmas Day, I roam up and down the halls and occasionally look out the windows at the snowy grounds, trees, and streets. A lone car drives along Third Street. Gerald rides on top of the car waving at me, slapping the car's roof and laughing. The car stops at the Mulberry Street intersection, and Gerald hops off and runs toward my door. He scoops up a snowball and lobs it toward my little window. It smashes against the glass right in front of my face. Then there's Gerald looking in at me, his face pressed against the glass until I step back and he fades in through the door, and steps toward me.

"Merry Christmas, bub!" he says. "Ready for a festive day of doing nothing?"

"However, it appears to you, I'm quite busy."

"Yes, yes, I know. Busy contemplating the Universe and missing your Maggie talks."

"Your acquisition of the obvious is commendable," I say.

"Well, are you ready for our little gift exchange?" he says, smiling.

I turn to walk away. "I didn't get you anything," I say.

"Awww, don't worry, chum. I do have a present for you."

"How nice," I say. "What could you possibly get me?"

"I've combed the far reaches of the Universe to get you something nice."

"All right. Thank you. When would you like to have our little exchange?" I ask.

"Later, my good friend, at the appropriate time."

"I know what it is," I say. "You're going to leave."

"Uh uh—I'm not saying anything until then."

"But I told you what I got you," I say.

"And it's much appreciated," he says. "I'm looking forward to nothing from you. How thoughtful."

"Thank you. At least warn me in advance when you're ready to give me mine so I can try to be in a good mood."

"Of course." he says, and then goes back outside in the snow.

I'll roam around for a while then. It's hard to be up for his antics when I'm moping around thinking about Maggie. When I find other things to occupy me, then it's all right. But today, I'm wondering what Maggie's doing, and is she happy? She has friends and will probably see them if the roads and sidewalks are passable. Gerald's mention of the Universe got me thinking. He gets me wondering about going outside. He doesn't hesitate to go out, but he's been going out for over a decade. I don't know if I'll go out for a while, but then I have a long time to practice avoiding detection. I head up to Maggie's classroom door. I always feel good here. Then I head down to the portraits. They're all in good shape. Gerald's been behaving himself. I gaze at the teachers, especially Miss Gould. I turn down the side hall and head east. When I pass the library, I stop to slide in. I browse the many books and after a couple of minutes, I freeze and stare at the shelf.

"Will you look at that!" I say. The book is staring right at me. *A History of Architecture*, just published this year.

I carefully lift it over to a table and open it.

"Prehistoric architecture to preclassical to Greek, Roman, Gothic, to modern, eastern. Wow, I did read about this book coming out and here it is!"

I spend hours reading through the book until I'm interrupted by Gerald who notices me in here.

"Well, there you are," he says. "I'm surprised you hadn't been in here yet. Ready to break for lunch?"

"Right," I say. "And I *have* been in here from time to time. So you finally decided to come in from the cold? Go take a hot bath or you'll catch your death of cold."

My attempt at humor is lost on him.

He smirks. "Aren't you going to ask me where I've been?"

"All right, where have you been?"

"Out and about in town," he says. "They've got Christmas lights up although they don't turn them on often because of the Wartime mandatory electricity restrictions but I did see them briefly last night. Still a lot of snow today and it's bitter cold, a record breaker I think. No one is out."

"But you were out."

"I didn't stay outside the whole time. I invited myself into the Oxford rooming home's living room. Maggie is doing well. She likes to read a lot. I've seen her several mornings curled up in a chair with a book this week. Today she had a new book, perhaps a Christmas present."

"A book is a nice gift," I say.

"She is probably longing to be in the arms of a gentleman, perhaps your arms if that were possible."

"Could be," I say, "but I'm sure she's content, enjoying her book today."

"Face it, you do have some kind of hold on her. I can't explain what it is you're doing."

"I'm not doing anything," I say.

"You must be. Maybe it's not intentional and you're not aware of it, but…"

"But what? After death speculation doesn't interest me. I'm glad she keeps my memory alive. I just hope she's happy and will be."

"There's a chance she will be happy. That's up to you."

"What do you mean, up to me?"

"Can't say."

"What were you saying about the Oxford?"

"They had lunch," he says, "then played games. Seems to be a daily occurrence for them since the heavy snow came. Maggie's got a couple of new friends, Norma and Hazel, both widows. They appear to enjoy one another's company, trading stories. Maggie seemed to enjoy the time, but I could sense her deep sadness."

"I still don't know what you're getting at," I say. "Being couped up inside when it's cold and snowy isn't for everyone, but I know Maggie's doing well from her talks to me."

"Then you need to get out more," Gerald says.

"To the Universe like you?"

"No, but you could see our vibrant town and watch its goings on, not to mention places beyond."

"How far away have you gone?" I ask.

"All around Kansas. Farthest is out to the chalk bluffs between Oakley and Scott City. They're magnificent. And I've also been to the boulder field north of Salina. Another area I like is the Gypsum Hills southwest of Wichita. And of course there's our Flint Hills. I stood atop Sugar Loaf in a thunderstorm last year in spring. A squall line passed over and I looked up into a rotating funnel cloud. It took all I had, but I managed to soar up in it. It was full of lightning and there were multiple vortices twisting around each other in it."

"Too bad it didn't draw you to the top," I say.

"Like you," he says, "no mass to grab on to. Like I said, it was all I could do to get up in it. It was low and skimmed the hill. And well, other places I can't omit include our State Capitol building. You'd love its architecture."

"French Renaissance," I say.

"That and its magnificent dome. I went to the upper walkway inside the dome. You might not like it up there, but it's a great place to walk with the view all the way down. And up in the cupola is fun."

"I've heard about those," I say, "I was never interested in the high up places there."

"I doubt you were, but things should be different for you now."

"I'm not sure about that, but yes, a lot of things are different now."

"For one, you don't have to shave or get a shave now, and other chores you don't have to worry about."

"Do me a favor and don't tell me this state of being is worth it for that."

"Then I'll leave you to your study." He shrugs and slips out of the library.

I go back to my book and start reading in the Eastern Architecture chapter about Korean Hanok architecture first introduced about 600 years ago. That design considers the positioning of a house in relation to its surroundings and seasons. I've read about that fellow, Frank Lloyd Wright, who's starting to use that concept.

January 25, 1919

Maggie

Paintings at an Exhibition

On Saturday afternoon, the soft roar of dozens of people greeted Maggie and Rose when they entered the building. They went to the gym and paid the fifteen-cent admission to the Art exhibition, then joined a crowd viewing over one hundred fifty of masterwork reproductions that were on display.

Maggie gazed around. "Aren't these wonderful?"

"So realistic," said Rose.

George Fielding approached. "Good afternoon, ladies," he said. "Great day for a fundraiser, isn't it? I think the spring-like weather brought people out."

Annie joined them. "Hello, Maggie, Rose, George," she said. "How are you all?"

George and Rose acknowledged her.

"I'm doing well," said Maggie. "And you? I'm just bracing for sympathy and advice."

"Well," said Annie, "Here comes Louise Pangborn."

"Oh, dear," said Maggie.

Louise stepped up to them. "Hello, everyone! Aren't these paintings marvelous?"

"They're very close matches to the originals," said Maggie.

"Aren't they, though?" Louise said.

"There's a fine art book in the library with full-color pictures of many of these."

"I've seen most of these in person," Louise said, "in the Louvre." She smiled and touched Rose's shoulder with her fingertips. "That's in Paris, France."

"Yes, I've been there, too," said Rose.

"Of course you have," said Louise. "I'm sure John took you, God rest his soul. How are you getting along?"

"Better without him."

"Oh." Louise turned to Maggie.

Uh oh, Maggie thought.

Louise reached over with her fingertips and tapped Maggie's arm. "And how are you holding up, dear?"

Annie stood behind Louise and made a face, pretending to hold up a heavy object.

Maggie almost burst out laughing.

"That poor boy," said Louise.

"I'm not surprised when the work was pushed as rapidly as possible," said Annie. "Bulletin boards not adequately secured to walls, things like that. Although, I realize it can take a few weeks for things to settle."

"No," said Louise, "I don't think Louie would hurry a job like this."

"Louie?" said Annie.

"Louie Mueller, the contractor," said Louise.

"I found an article from last year that mentioned pushing work as rapidly as possible," insisted Annie.

"All right," Louise said, turning to George. "And Mr. Fielding, you're as handsome as ever. Out without your wedding ring, I see?"

"Mrs. Fielding had him leave it at home so he can flirt with the ladies," said Annie.

George smiled, embarrassed. "Mrs. Fielding will be along shortly. My ring's at the jeweler being repaired."

"Oh, now," said Louise. "Well, you all enjoy the art show." She turned and left.

"What a card." said Annie, laughing.

"I was also wondering about pushing for rapid completion," said Rose. "I remember reading about that, too. If Louise is right about the contractor, it makes sense any new building could have loose fixtures. I'm so glad you weren't hurt, Annie."

Maggie watched Louise leave the gym. "I think I'll get up on the stage and announce: 'Ladies and gentlemen, I am fine! Ricky was a good friend!'" she said.

Annie pointed to the stage. "It's open, Maggie!"

"Wait," said Maggie, pointing to the stage. "Look, they're rolling out a piano."

Miss Hoffman stepped onto the stage, sat at the piano and started to play.

"Nice to have music fill the gym," said Rose.

Maggie smiled. "Let's go view some reproductions."

They wandered around the perimeter of the gym for a while then decided where to join several teachers who had gathered around some displays in front of the stage.

They reached those displays; two teachers stood talking next to a couple of paintings and Ruby Francis, the art teacher was explaining something about one of the paintings.

She gestured to a landscape scene and turned to Maggie. "Look at this one by Claude Monet, *Wild Poppies Near Argenteuil.* Doesn't that look like our countryside around Eureka?"

Maggie leaned toward it and gazed at the scene of reddish-orange poppies on a grassy hillside with a few trees on the hilltop and background, and with a woman carrying an umbrella accompanying a young girl holding flowers.

"Why yes," said Maggie. "It does!" She turned to Rose and Annie. "Do you like the impressionism style?"

"It's all right," said Rose.

"It's fabulous if you have blurry vision," said Annie.

"Well," said Maggie, "I read Monet's eyesight isn't what it used to be, but I think this was painted in the 1870s."

"With that style, his eyesight wouldn't have to be good," said Annie.

Ruby stepped back. "Every time a new art form emerges, it has detractors," she said.

Maggie peered at another painting near the Monet work, one of a woman in a blue and white dress assisting a young person seated at a desk holding a page of a book while the woman tapped it with a pointing object. "Oh, what's that work called?" Maggie asked.

Ruby smiled. "It's *The Teacher* by Jean Baptiste Simeon."

"Very nice. When was it painted?"

"Around 1740. Notice the style difference between it and that one after it, *The Reluctant Courtship* by Henry Andrews, which was a mid-nineteenth century panting. Maybe it's just me, but I think placement is important and best not have *The Teacher* next to the Henry Andrews work. I'm not sure who moved them, but I wouldn't have placed them like that."

Maggie stepped back and gazed at the two paintings side by side. "I would," she said.

February 18, 1919

Ricky

I mosey around the halls, but not so much on the second-floor main hallway, my usual favorite area to pace. I've been poking around places to stay away from Gerald who's trying to take over all my favorite locations. I'm looking for more places, except I like walking by Maggie's classroom often, so I've come up with a route that takes me to the boiler room, to the first floor, the gym, stage, some of the grade school classes, the hallways, the accident location and sometimes I peek into the principal's office. I still encounter Gerald sometimes, since I cover so much area, but today I manage to avoid him so far. My fondness for the accident location grows, because Maggie goes there to talk to me. This makes it special and it's losing its negative aspect for me.

Now, here comes Gerald. I go over by the stairway, because I don't want him near where Maggie talks to me. He's already intruded too much on her places. I don't need to give him a reason to intrude on her more.

He comes toward me. "Hi, Slacker Rick. What's new?"

"You're not new."

"Do you know what today is?"

"I think it's mid-week, because classes are being held."

"Day of week isn't important. It's February eighteenth, your one-year anniversary."

"I don't pay attention to dates, but the passage of time seems less."

"Your perception is different. Welcome to Infinity."

"I don't like it. Do you?" I say.

"Nope, but with years of death experience, I'm an entity of the world, which is more than I can say for you who doesn't want to get out."

"Once again, you're trying to rehash an argument we've already settled."

"No we haven't, because you continue to barricade yourself behind an imaginary barrier."

"It's not imaginary. I've explained it."

"I've been trying to convince you, but you're too dense to get it. I'll lay it on the line."

"I don't believe you."

"I promise my intentions are good, but you're like a squatter here."

"Squatter, nothing. I paid for this place and got you added to my debt."

"Would you like to have your debt forgiven?"

"What do you mean? I want straight, unambiguous language."

"All right. Here it is—you know how I've been after you to stop interfering and helping people."

"Yes and I know why."

"No, you don't."

"Come on."

"All right. Listen. How would you like to be rid of me forever?"

"You mean you would leave?"

He turns to walk away. "No, *you* would."

* * *

Later, the bell rings, the bell rings, letting the last class of the day out, so I duck behind this hall's radiator.

Students pour out of the classrooms and flow out the exits.

A few minutes later, Maggie goes to the accident location as the hallway clears.

"Ricky," she says, "I wasn't going to stop here tonight, but it's been one year since your accident and that has awakened old thoughts, causing me to relive the what-might-have-beens. I've thought of writing all this down in a diary, but I don't need to. The memories are strong, including those before your accident. You know what I did on Sunday afternoon? I looked at houses for sale, just for fun. Of course, most are too expensive for me, but I like to think what might have been if we would have been together and bought one of the cute little ones. I hope I don't frighten you by talking about that. Meanwhile, we had a nice art exhibit fundraiser for the school. I was particularly interested in a coincidence of two paintings next to each other that Ruby Francis said were not placed there intentionally.

"I'm glad this year so far is more normal than the disastrous last year. I have a good group of students and they're doing well, considering what they've been through. I'm looking forward to spring after some of the brutal winter days we've had.

"I wish you could really hear me. I wish you could tell me all of what you thought when you were alive. Your interests and your thoughts about us. I thank you for your thoughts to me before the accident. I never tire of reading the letter you wrote on your last day with us, and the card holder remains my most cherished possession.

"What's really strange and wonderful is how close I feel to you when I'm in this location. Not only right here, but also up by my classroom. Up there, it's as if you're standing outside my door waiting for me. I wonder how long this feeling will last. I hope it never goes away."

March 15, 1919

Ricky

"Will people notice us in this rain?" I ask Gerald.

"Not really," he says, "just keep most of your body hidden in the mailbox for the moment, and then we can go up onto the porch and you can sit there and relive the pre-accident days at your old rooming house for a while."

"I didn't expect that. I'd love to do that. We should have come here on a weekday so I could watch Maggie walk by."

Gerald points over to the Oxford where Maggie emerges onto the porch with an umbrella.

"Let's get up the steps," I say.

"Follow me like this," he says, blending into the ground as he slides across the grass next to the sidewalk and slides up onto the steps to the porch.

I'm careful since it's daytime. Getting here from the school was easy before dawn. I mimic his method and make it onto the porch. Gerald is sitting with his back against the wall. He pats the floor next to him. Does that mean we're friends now? Well, if he's trying to be then I won't refute it. I slide over and sit with my back against the wall about two feet from him.

I watch over toward Maggie's rooming home and she is on the sidewalk walking this way holding her umbrella against the wind to keep it from inverting. Despite the wind and rain, it appears pleasant out, as people aren't wearing heavy coats, many carrying umbrellas aimed against the wind gusts, others holding onto their hats and gripping tight their raincoats.

Maggie takes control of her umbrella and strolls past, glancing up toward where I'm sitting. As she passes by, she waves and smiles.

That warms my emotions.

"Gerald," I say. "Did she see me?"

"Don't be silly. Of course not. You're nothing to her."

"Don't say that!"

"You know what I mean."

We lean forward and watch her walk on.

"Do you want to walk along with her?"

"That would be a dream, but no. Let's let her be."

"She won't know. Although maybe you shouldn't do that now and should sharpen your skills for being out and about first to ensure you're not seen. Do that and you'll walk with her soon enough."

Benny comes out to the porch with Perry, whom I didn't know well and they sit in the wooden chairs.

"Boy howdy," Benny says, "it's so warm out today. Too bad it's raining."

"It feels as warm outside as it does inside," Perry says, pulling his hat tighter and stretching his legs out as he leans back.

Benny looks down the sidewalk at Maggie receding. "There she goes," he says.

"Who?" Perry asks.

"Maggie Stilwell, teaches at Mulberry."

"The gal who caught Ricky's interest?"

"That's the one," Benny says. "She was interested in him, too," He clasps his fingers behind his head.

"Too bad about him," Perry says. "He seemed like a decent fellow."

"He was. I got to know him. His main flaw was not acting on his desires. They could have been a couple."

"Well," Perry says, looking down the sidewalk at her walking away, "seeing how it's been a year or so since he died and I'm unattached..."

"Forget it," Benny says.

"Why? Is she still stuck on Ricky?"

"Maybe," Benny says, "but I'm unattached, too. She would be quite a catch and I've known her longer. Too few men appreciate her as attractive, and that's all the better for me."

"Don't be too sure. I've heard talk about her," Perry says.

"If she stops mourning Ricky," Benny says, "then I'm claiming her."

"Oh, so you're the rightful heir to the 'prize'?" Perry says.

Benny shakes his head. "I didn't mean that."

"Sounded like it. She deserves respect and I suspect she will only entertain courting attempts from men who treat her such."

"You're as naïve as Ricky was."

Gerald turns to me. "These things are what you're missing by staying behind your barricade at the school."

"Men will always say things," I say. "Perry seems all right, but I admit my emotional state is affected, and it hurts when he compliments her. Am I being selfish by being jealous?"

"Perhaps. Maybe you'll have to contemplate that."

"I just want to look forward to Maggie's talks."

Gerald points down Main Street to Maggie crossing over toward the courthouse block.

She walks along the sidewalk by the gazebo. A man steps from it holding an umbrella and tips his hat at her. The man gestures his hand toward the gazebo to invite her to join him there. After he goes in, she stands under the roof overhang out of the rain. The man appears very animated. Maggie stays and talks for a bit then goes back to the sidewalk and heads south along Main Street, keeping her umbrella positioned while sticking close to the buildings' awnings as she fades into the distance.

A few hours later, after Benny and Perry have gone about other activities, Gerald and I finish our intermittent discussions and arguing and prepare to go back to Mulberry School under protection of late evening. It's still raining, but that won't affect us.

Something catches my attention a couple of blocks down Main Street. A man and woman huddled beneath an umbrella are walking this way. As they draw closer, I discover that is Maggie with a man and—I can't help it—that hurts.

They reach us, and Gerald says, "Don't avert your attention. Pay attention to who he is."

I reluctantly comply and find that the man is George Fielding.

"I sense recognition and relief in you," Gerald says.

"He's another teacher at Mulberry," I say. "He's married and I have no suspicions about him."

Maggie and George continue to the Oxford, and he bids goodbye as she walks up the steps.

"Admit it, you felt enormous jealousy," says Gerald.

"It's true. I know I should only want happiness for Maggie, but I'm only human."

"Human? Are you?"

"I was."

He jabs me. "Do you miss it?"

"What do you think?" I say, batting his hand away. "Don't you miss it?"

"Yes, but I didn't have a choice."

March 18, 1919

Ricky

"You're doing fine," Gerald says a few evenings later as we stand on the front steps outside the main entrance to the school. "You're mostly invisible, just a wrinkle. And you know what?"

"What?" I say.

"When you move, you fade more. Like when you tripped Jackie to save him from jumping on the side horse."

"After you moved it there," I say.

He starts to walk out to the sidewalk on Mulberry Street "Anyway, let's go downtown."

"What for?"

"Maggie left a bit ago," he says. "Let's go see what she's up to."

"As I said before, I prefer to let her be."

"Well then," he says, walking away toward Third Street.

He's trying to manipulate me. I watch his wrinkle continue on.

Oh all right! I'll go with him. "Gerald! Wait up!"

He stops and waits, barely visible. I catch up. "Where exactly are we going?" I ask.

"The courthouse gazebo," he says as we start walking.

"Why there?"

"To see if Maggie goes there."

"Why does that matter?"

"Don't you know?"

"It's a nice gazebo," I say.

"And a town tradition. Oh, I forgot you didn't live here long. When a couple has their first kiss there, they seal their relationship as courting, perhaps more."

"Why do you think she's going there?"

"You have to ask? We need to see if she's meeting anyone. She left earlier than usual today. Notice how she didn't stop at the accident location and talk to you before she left?"

"She doesn't always," I say. "She has things to do. As a teacher, she's very busy."

"Let's go," he says, and we pick up the pace. We head west on Third toward downtown, down the small hill, past Houston Lumber, and reach Main Street.

"There she is," says Gerald, pointing to the gazebo.

"So what?" I say. "She's at the gazebo. All alone with a book."

"Alone for now. We can wait. A man might meet her there."

"I don't want to spy on her," I say.

"I'm going over there. You can stay here," he says, crosses Main, and goes to the gazebo. I watch his wrinkle stand next to the railing facing in. Maggie sits there reading her book, sometimes looking around. Gerald keeps watching her from just a few feet. I wish he'd leave her alone. I don't think she's waiting for anyone, but I guess she could be and if she is, no matter how it affects me, I hope she's happy whatever she does.

Gerald faces me and yells across. "Ricky, get over here!"

Now what? "What is it!" I yell back.

"She's talking! You need to hear this!"

Now he's got me curious, so I cross Main and join him.

Maggie has stopped talking by the time I get there.

"What?" I say.

Maggie takes out her card holder.

"She was talking to you!" he says. "Why don't you go in and sit next to her?"

"No. Don't tempt me. I'd like to, but being next to her will make parting sadder. I can listen from here."

Maggie brought the card holder to her lips. "Ricky," she says. Gerald nudges me with an elbow. "I'm wondering about if we had met here, even if by accident, or if I arranged it or tricked you into showing up here, what would have happened? Maybe we'd have had a nice talk, gotten to know each other, and gotten over our mutual shyness. And then, who knows?" She closes her book and brings the card holder back to her lips.

"That's it!" Gerald says.

"Her desire to meet?" I say.

"No, the card holder. It's the link that keeps her attached to you. You planned it well, boy. Leave the card holder to her, have your cousin pass letters to her and you've got a hold on her just in case."

"You act as if it was intentional, that those things can pull her along," I say. "That's ridiculous, and I had no such intention when I was alive. I just wanted her to know how I felt."

"And yet, you never approached her, but don't underestimate the things you can do after you're gone."

"I was about to approach her, but that stupid accident happened. What do you mean, 'things I can do?'"

"Just wait."

"Wait for what?"

Gerald changes the subject. "You have to admit that card holder has her attached to your memory."

"It seems to," I say.

"She feels your presence at school. Probably here, too," he says. "Look at her."

Maggie has folded her arms over her chest and closes her eyes. She takes a handkerchief to her eyes, puts her book and card holder in her bag, and gets up to go cross Main Street. She goes to the crosswalk and strolls across, reaches into her bag, and appears to gasp as she fumbles around in it. She turns around abruptly to head back to the gazebo. A car screeches to a stop barely missing her. The driver gets out and goes to her. She's apologizing for not paying attention. He dismisses that and wants to be sure she's all right. She hurries back to the gazebo and is frantic as she searches for something.

"What is it?" I say. "I'm worried about this."

"I don't know. Did she lose the card holder?"

"Apparently," I say. "I didn't notice if she dropped it or not."

She sits and digs in her bag. "Oh!" she says pulling out a money purse. She sighs and glances around then gets up and goes over to the opposite sidewalk, turning up toward the Oxford.

"As much as we discuss interference, would you save her if she were about to die in a mishap if you could?"

"Of course I would!" I say.

"All right, let's go back to the school. I've got something to discuss about that."

* * *

We return to the school and meet outside Maggie's classroom.

"You saw how Maggie escaped getting hit," he says. "Now, Ricky, you are being given a choice. Consider it carefully."

Gerald continues—

You have a chance to save Maggie during a mishap, accident, what have you."

"Option one. Let her die, you and she get another chance to start a life together a year ago and you avoid the accident.

"Option two. Save her, you both continue on as you are now.

"Consider it."

"How am I to consider such a strange choice?"

"Remember that gift I promised you at Christmas? This is your advance notice."

My gift? This? I don't know how to take this weird turn of things.

Gerald smiles, then leaves me alone next to the radiator in the hallway outside Maggie's classroom. This intellectual exercise is one I'm not prepared for. I enjoy Maggie's talks and want to continue to bask in that, and yet now I have this crazy hypothetical to ponder.

* * *

Two days later, I roam around the dim halls trying to think about my usual topics: Maggie and her talks, and my hopes for her wellbeing, but thoughts keep returning to options Gerald mentioned. What am I supposed to think? He's a constant irritant and I don't know what to do about that. He's teasing me, but perhaps some self-analysis with his little hypothetical might be useful.

I go to the accident scene.

He said to think about the two choices. I rehash them in my mind.

One option: Let her die, and we both get a second chance.

The other option: Save her, and we both go on as we are now, nothing changes.

Well, if I save her, and she goes on with life, she might eventually heal and accept that I'm gone. She might meet someone and be happy. I have to suppress my jealousy even thinking about that, but she would be happy. In the meantime, with that option, I'll go on as I am now, roaming endlessly around the school, but maybe Gerald is right that I can enjoy going outside more and experience the world. I could be with Maggie in a sense, but not really with her, and she would get nothing out of that.

The thought of starting over is exceedingly alluring, but the thought of letting her die isn't.

But what if Maggie and I *could* start over?

Would it be for *my* happiness or *hers* or both if she dies and we get to start over? Will a second chance *benefit* Maggie and me both? Would she *want* to go back and start over? Maybe, but would it be selfish of me to make that decision? Then again, we'd at least get a chance we'd both desire.

I wish Gerald would stop teasing me. He says it's real, but he hits me right where it hurts. Do I trust him? I'm going to abandon the puzzle for now.

Now he comes around the corner and approaches.

"Why are you mocking me?" I ask.

"Mocking? Of course not, dear fellow," he says. "I'm giving you more to fill your time."

I turn away from him. "You don't have to keep teasing me."

Gerald turns to walk away. "Wrong again…this is real. You'll get one chance."

March 22, 1919

Ricky

I walk to Second and Mulberry Streets and down Second in the direction of downtown. I am enjoying a new freedom Gerald taught me by getting outside. Mulberry School will always be home, whatever Gerald claims as his own domain. But now I can get out and experience the world again in whatever ways I can in this state of being. The spring flowers are starting to bud. I pass by a large house on the corner to my right with a row of daffodils sprouting in front of the porch. The trees are budding as well. The daffodils will have flowers in a couple of weeks, which reminds me I have things to look forward to and I don't have to have an infinite bland existence. With spring brings lightened moods of people, kids looking forward to summer, some of them preparing to graduate, and some women and men wearing new spring outfits. Maggie always looks nice and I expect she'll have something nice to wear as the weather warms. She'll probably hit a spring sale or two and I hope she'll be happy when she finishes another school year of bringing students along in their education. She must derive great satisfaction from that.

I only wish I could experience that joy with her and I start thinking about my so-called choices that Gerald "offered" as I continue down the little hill. If I hang around her and stay nearby, I could, as Gerald suggests, be with her in a sense. But I don't want to stalk her, and

199

as I keep telling Gerald: let her be. I can derive satisfaction in her accomplishments. But then, will she *really* be happy? She still clutches the card holder and talks to me. I get happiness from that, but is that sad and frustrating for her?

The choice is wearing on my emotions, so I abandon the thoughts for the moment and try to enjoy nature around me.

Down the hill, on my left a brick bungalow—or is that a craftsman—has peonies growing in front of the porch. I should know the style of house with my architecture knowledge. I stop and gaze at the house. It's a craftsman, judging by the style of the square brick columns on the porch. A nice look and I can imagine an interior of fine woodwork and a good layout. Gerald was right. Getting out is fun. I could spend years cataloging all the houses in Eureka. To what end? My own enjoyment.

A man and woman emerge onto the porch, the man with a rake, the woman with a hoe, and they set to work getting their yard ready for spring.

I don't want to be spotted, so I pick up the pace and pass School Street with a large two-story house on the corner with a wraparound porch. A foursquare house, I believe. It also has flowers lining the porch on the Second and School Street sides. Eureka is heading toward an attractive spring of colors and foliage, again that's something to look forward to.

At the bottom the hill, I cross Elm Street and pass between a foursquare and bungalow adorning the corners and I reach the edge of downtown. On Main Street, I walk along the Opera House Block and look around at the businesses. They're still there. It's only been a year since I was last here, after all, so I would expect them to be. I pause in front of one of the shops and look around at the busy Main Street, at the Model Ts, Pontiacs, and occasional Packards puttering up and down and people going in and out of shops and the Royal Café with diners entering. It's nice to see all the bustling activity.

Something down on First and Main catches my attention. A crowd has gathered at the intersection. The police have it blocked off. I assume there's an accident and make my way there. No cars are present, perhaps towed away already. As I sneak to a gap in the surrounding spectators, I notice a police officer on his hands and knees looking down a gaping construction hole, calling to someone. Worried workers mill around.

"She was distracted," someone says.

"The poor dear. She was," someone else says.

The officer shouts down the hole. "Miss Stilwell! Can you hear me! We're here to get you out!"

Maggie!

Another officer says they need special extraction equipment.

Never mind invisibility: I zoom over to the construction hole and peer down. There's Maggie! Badly hurt!

My choices from Gerald—*No time for that.*

I dive down the hole.

I won't let you die, dear Maggie!

Her legs are broken; a rock is wedged on her shoulder, trapping her. I summon all my strength so I can heave the rock from her. She's almost in shock and she needs those rescuers *now*. I lean over her.

She reaches a shaky hand toward me. "Ricky."

Maggie

Maggie started out early from the Oxford Rooming House on North Main Street and paused on the sidewalk out front to check her timing. She gazed down to another rooming house a few buildings ahead. Ricky was on the porch settled on a chair with his coffee, so she pinched her cheeks and started along the sidewalk. When she passed by his porch, her eyes met his; she smiled and waved, wiggling her fingers. Ricky waved back and smiled, then his housemate, Benny emerged from the front door and smiled at her. She gave a polite smile back and continued on. Several blocks later, she glanced back and noticed Ricky and Benny stepping off the porch to go to the construction site. She continued to Fourth Street and headed east toward the high school.

She arrived at the school later and went into the teachers' lounge. George Fielding stood when she entered the room. "Good morning, Miss Stilwell," he said, pointing to a side table. "Fresh coffee."

"Thank you, Mr. Fielding. Any news here?"

"Not much," he said. "Just that Principal Fuller wants to meet with you sometime about the move to the new Mulberry Street school."

"Good. I have some questions," said Maggie. She glanced at the clock. "Well, I'll get on up to my class. Have a good day, Mr. Fielding." She hung up her coat, clutched her purse and started to leave.

"Have another good day in the penthouse," he said.

She hopped up the stairs and entered her makeshift classroom. Her students waited for her to begin.

"Well, you'll soon be in the new school," she said. "We're supposed to move over in three weeks. The workmen are finishing some of the rooms, but we're being allowed to move in early!"

Her students applauded.

One student raised her hand. "Miss Stilwell? What will our classes be like?"

"Well, my English classroom will be on the second floor over on the west side. The classrooms are quite modern. The other Junior High classes will be on that floor, too. Of course, you all will be back in this building next year."

Their happy expressions fell.

"But," Maggie continued, "you'll be in real classrooms again."

Applause once more.

"All right," she said, "let's get started." She went to the chalkboard. She wrote the day's reading assignment and allowed the students to read it in class for the rest of the hour.

When the lunch hour arrived, she left the building and hurried to Mulberry Street to watch from Third Street as some workers exited the new building. She tried to spot Ricky, but he wasn't with the others. His friend Benny was about to get into a car with another worker when he noticed her and waved. She waved back and he motioned to her to stay put. She remained on the corner until the car drove over to her and stopped.

"Say, Miss Stilwell," Benny said, leaning out the window. "Would you like to join us for lunch?"

"Well…" she said.

"We're going to the Royal Café," he said. "They have fast service and we'll give you a ride back to the high school afterwards."

"Well, all right," she said.

Benny hopped out and helped her settle into the back seat.

"How was work today for you fellas?" she asked.

"It was swell," Benny said. "We got a lot done today, and you'll be pleased when you move in." He pointed to the driver. "I believe you know Marcus."

"Yes, nice to see you again, Marcus," she said. "That's wonderful about the school."

"Do you want to know how it went for Ricky?" Marcus said, smiling.

"Yes, how was his first day?" she asked, knowing they were going to try to get her to reveal her feelings for him. "Why didn't he come with you guys? Did he get delayed?"

"No," Benny said. "He's meeting us there."

"Oh!" Maggie felt a nervous jab to her stomach. "How nice."

"He got the best job of all," Benny said.

"Errand boy," Marcus said.

"No," Benny said. "Stanchfield said that to distract us from the good job they offered him. When he returned to the school around ten-thirty he told me about it."

"I'm glad for him," Maggie said.

"Ricky must have impressed Mr. Mueller when he and Stanchfield went to the downtown office," Benny said. "I'll get the dirt this evening."

They arrived at the Royal Café where Ricky was inside waiting for them. When Maggie walked in with them, Ricky straightened up and acted nonchalant. When her eyes met his, she tried not to avert her gaze as did he.

"Hello, Maggie," he said, nodding. "Nice to see you."

"And you, Ricky. "It was a spur of the moment decision when these gentlemen drove by me."

"Right," Marcus said, "we saw Maggie heading for town and offered."

"We'd better go seat ourselves," Benny said.

Maggie's and Ricky's attentions turned toward the dining parlor and Benny leaned over to Marcus. "Ready?" he whispered.

"Ready," Marcus replied.

They found a rectangular table. Benny held a chair out for Maggie and she went to it. Benny gave a nod to Marcus.

Ricky took the seat across from her after Marcus took the other seat on that side.

Benny sat next to Maggie, scooting his chair over a bit away from hers.

"Well," Benny said. "The sandwiches here are fine and come quickly."

"That sounds good to me," said Maggie.

"Yes," said Benny. "Marcus and I will treat you both."

"Well," said Ricky. "You don't have—"

"We insist," Marcus said.

"Thank you, gentlemen," said Maggie.

"Thank you from me, too," said Ricky.

Their orders arrived quickly, true to the Royal Café's reputation, and the four of them started enjoying their lunch.

Maggie was mostly quiet, glancing at Ricky a few times as he ate slowly and also didn't say much until Benny started talking.

"Say, Ricky," Benny said, "what is your new job like?"

"Mr. Mueller has me looking over blueprints for a future addition to the high school," replied Ricky. "It's quite interesting."

"So Stanchfield saying he needed an errand boy was a cover up," Marcus said.

"Not really," said Ricky. "Mr. Mueller grabbed me away from him." Ricky stopped talking about it then and glanced at Maggie. "How was your morning at school?"

"Very good. We get to move into the new school in next week. My students are thrilled and I am, too."

"Let me know if you have any issues when you move in," Benny said.

"Thank you," she said, a bit embarrassed.

Ricky gave a nervous smile to Maggie which she returned.

February 18, 1918

Gerald

On the same morning, I walk into a spot of nothingness near Ricky's would-be accident location. "Where am I?" I say.

"You are here," a voice says.

"Did it happen?" I ask.

"Yes."

"I assume I did all right."

"Your efforts have been fine," the voice says.

"I never told Ricky of my scheming to keep Maggie interested," I say.

"Your comment to Ricky at the gazebo about the card holder attaching her to him was partially correct as you helped make that connection along the way."

"Yes," I say proudly. "Are they now back to before he died?"

"Yes, they arrived just before that time."

"Does he face the same events again?"

"Mostly."

"If so, Ricky will always remember me as misleading him if it's different this time," I say.

"No. He and Maggie have no memory of the *before*."

"What now?" I ask.

"You are free to reclaim your domain. Take a lesson from Ricky. He helped people. Go on now."

I step into the first-floor main hallway. Ricky is there with several men standing next to scaffolding, including Bart Stanchfield in bib overalls.

"You're Ricky?" Stanchfield asks.

"Yes, sir," Ricky says. "I'm ready to work."

"Of course you are," Stanchfield says. "Are you sure you can do this kind of work?" He looks Ricky up and down.

"Yes, sir," Ricky says. "Whatever you need me to do."

"Let's get started," Stanchfield says.

"Sir," Ricky says, "it looks like the schoolhouse is nearly complete."

Stanchfield gestures toward the ceiling above the scaffolding. "We have some work on the ceiling to finish up," he says.

The scaffolding has three bound-wood plank platforms, each suspended with cables from the one above it with ladders between them. The ladders from one angles up to the next platform and another leads to the upper platform.

"We need to secure that light fixture," Stanchfield says, pointing to a white globe suspended by electrical wires from a freshly varnished cross beam. He then points to a worker near Ricky. "This is Cheney. He has your tools and he's in charge of this area."

Ricky looks up and around at the upper scaffolding. It's high up there. He looks hesitant.

"Get a-going, boy," Stanchfield says. "We're on a schedule. Mr. Mueller wants this part done today." He shakes his head and steps away.

Cheney turns toward Ricky and chuckles. "Welcome to the Cranky Stanchfield club," he says as he hands a tool belt to Ricky. "First day here?"

Ricky nods.

"Well, better get to it if you don't want today to be your last day."

Ricky secures the tool belt and starts to reach for the ladder.

I dive toward him and knock him over.

The other guys burst out in laughter and Stanchfield breaks it up.

"You clumsy oaf," Stanchfield says. "Get up and get out of the way so a capable man can get up there."

Ricky stands up while Benny steps forward.

"I'll go up, Mr. Stanchfield," Benny says.

"All right," Stanchfield says. "Austin, you're just not cut out for this, but you seem eager, and I need an errand boy." That is met with chuckles from the others.

"Shut up," Stanchfield says. "He won't make as much as you guys, but he'll do all right."

"Thank you, sir," Ricky says.

"Can you drive, son? And do you have a driver's license?"

"Yes sir."

"All right then. Mr. Mueller has a temporary office in the Crebo building downtown. Come and drive me there. I have some things for you to do." He turns to Cheney. "Take over here."

Stanchfield puts his hand onto Ricky's shoulder, and they head for the front doors.

Ricky glances back at the scaffolding. Benny has already scaled it and is working on the light fixture.

Stanchfield also glances back. "Take it easy up there, Hodges," he calls up. "We don't need an accident here."

"All right, sir," Benny replies.

Stanchfield and Ricky leave the building.

I watch the workers for a moment then glance toward the open front doors as Ricky and Stanchfield walk away. "Glad you made the correct decision saving Maggie," I say. "Good luck, fella. I owed you this."

Eric T. Reynolds

I leave the main hallway and relish my upcoming solitude as I go upstairs to the second-floor main hallway. I go by the door that will be Maggie's classroom and peek in. It's empty now, ready for desks and a chalkboard and window shades to be installed, but it will soon have those and the caring touch of a brilliant teacher with her eager students at the desks.

"Follow your dreams, Ricky," I say. "Be brave— Maggie isn't as terrifying as being up on scaffolding. Quite the contrary."

March 9, 1918

Gerald

I have my coveted solitude except for some workers, but I need to think about things.

Ricky and Maggie got to start over. He made the right decision so he's gone from here, but I actually miss the bumbling ol' fool. He did all right, despite being told that the opposite would give them a second chance. She had no choice in the matter.

I have infinity to mull over if it was evenly fair to both Maggie and Ricky. If the living world could know about this, then it could be discussed by scholars for years to come.

Meanwhile, I'll drift around my schoolhouse home, not to mention the town, and relish the times when no people are in here.

For infinity. But what's that mean? If Today is good, then an infinity of good days is...good. Since I've mastered getting out in the world, I'll witness the advancement of the species to which I used to belong. I've already watched advances from this state of being for over a decade. Automobiles are incredible now. Some specially designed for racing can go sixty miles an hour! I can remember when it was believed that no one could survive at such a speed.

I'll plan to take the advice and follow Ricky's example to help people, but I don't think there'll be anything wrong with having some fun along the way. If I cause some "manifestations," then I'll enjoy the reactions from wary people. *Boo!*—Hahaha.

And there's Ricky…I just didn't realize it, but we "met" before when he was a fourth grader at Eastside grade school in spring of 1904.

* April 1904 *

I figured out how to go be around people without being seen by them so when I heard kids and their screaming play outside, I went out to Eastside's playground, and encountered kids of all ages. On the swing set full of kids, some of them flew high in their forward arcs. The teeter totter had three times the kids for which it was designed. About a dozen kids were playing on the ladders and high bars. One kid who looked about nine was hanging by his hands trying to hurry his way across the high bar.

"Come on, Ricky! You have to get to the other side before I get to tensies!" a girl yelled.

He moved as fast as he could and just before he reached the end of the bar—

The girl yelled, "Awww, Ricky!"

Ricky grabbed the end crossbar and shimmied over to the ladder. He looked disappointed as did the girl while another girl and boy shouted success. When Ricky reached the ground, he moseyed around the base of the structure, gazing up at it, holding his hands up in a formation as if to analyze the bar connections and overall structure.

I went over near him.

Rumbles abounded of kids saying, "Look at him, what's he doing?" Followed by laughter.

A boy ran over to Ricky and grabbed his hands, pulling them down.

"Hey," Ricky said.

"You look like a goof," the boy said.

Ricky shrugged. "I've never been good at bar-jacks."

"That's why it's hard to get girls to play with you."

"You mean play bar-jacks with me," said Ricky.

The boy laughed. "Then what are you good at?"

"Lots."

Ricky and the boy, standing about a foot apart were facing the bars and ladders play structure, so I went between them and put a hand on each back to nudge them forward. It worked. Each thought the other was putting a friendly hand on his back and they walked, still friends.

"Look!" the boy shouted.

A small girl was high up on the bar hanging by fingers. Ricky ran over below her just as she lost her grip and she fell into his arms. The other kids ran over to them and offered congratulatory pats on the back. Ricky eased the girl down. She sniffled, but was all right.

His bar-jacks partner jumped up and ran to him. "Our hero!"

* * *

I should have reminisced that with him when he was here rather than torment him for reasons I thought were valid. I'm sure I'll think of many more things I've done or not done that I regret with infinity to think about them.

Well, my solitude is over for the moment. Somebody's opening the front doors.

Maggie is coming in with a box of things. She's happy and excited, judging by her expression.

Maggie, pardon me if I slide around and follow you for a while.

Maggie balances the box on her knee and proceeds up the stairs to the landing, then stops and catches her breath.

A breeze rushes in through the open doors below, and a far-off classroom door slams shut. When Ricky was here, he could have gotten blamed for that. Maggie gasps and continues on. A moment later, somebody emerges from a hallway below and calls up to her. "All right if I close these doors!"

"That's fine! Thank you!" she replies.

She carries the box up the last flight and goes along the locker-lined hall to her classroom on the left. The room and its shiny wood floors greet her; she draws in a breath through her nose to take in the smell of fresh wall paint and shellac on the wood trim. School staff has arranged the desks in neat rows. Her big wooden desk sits at the front with a green chalkboard on the north wall behind it. The board is fresh and new, devoid of any chalk use. A fresh box of chalk sits at one end of the board tray next to a couple of new erasers. Someone on staff has placed portraits of Washington and Lincoln leaning against the wall beneath the board. She sets the box down next to the desk and pulls out a book.

She looks around the room, and I think she's impressed with everything so modern. She turns to the chalkboard, takes out a new piece of chalk, and smiles. On the middle of the board, she writes, "Miss Stilwell, 8th Grade English." She then goes back to her desk and the box to put the items away into a drawer. A few moments later, she goes out across the wide hallway, walks down the narrower side hall, and peeks into the first room on the left. A teacher is arranging his desk.

"Hello, Miss Stilwell," he says, looking up.

"Mr. Fielding?" she says. "You'll be teaching here now?"

"Apparently I'm shifting from geometry back to eight grade math. Seems I'm needed more here than at the high school."

"It'll be nice to have you here."

He smiles and nods. "Say, I don't mean to intrude, but you're sure looking joyful, and if I may ask, are you getting more acquainted with that young man, Ricky Austin? You seem content, or should I say, 'hopeful'."

"Interested, and maybe I'd say, hopeful," she says.

"Getting ready for Monday?" he asks.

"My students are excited to move out of that awful third floor of the high school."

"As are the grade school kids excited to get into the new school," he said.

"It'll be great to see their eager faces when they arrive, won't it?" Maggie smiles and excuses herself to leave, continuing along the hallway past another classroom on the left, then to the restrooms. She steps into the girls' restroom for a moment.

"What nice modern fixtures and plumbing," she mutters when she exits.

She returns to her room and looks around once more then heads downstairs to leave the building, walking with a spring in her step.

March 25, 1918

Ricky

Louie Mueller sat back in his chair and puffed on a cigar. "Well, son, you ready for the school dedication?"

"I admit I'm nervous," said Ricky. "I've never gotten up in front of an audience before."

"Well, it's less frightening than other things," Mueller said, laughing.

"Very true," Ricky said, chuckling.

"Now then, you'll be up after State Superintendent Ross gives his address. I assume you've prepared a short speech?"

"Yes, I have," said Ricky. "I hope it's all right."

"Speak from the heart, boy. You'll do fine. So this is more than you expected, is it? You could be climbing ladders and scaffolding."

"No, thank you. I'd get dizzy and fall, sure as the world."

"We don't want that. Anyway, just practice your delivery."

* * *

That evening, Ricky wore his gray suit and a new shirt and tie. He sat in one of the chairs near the stage along with other presenters. He tried not to pay attention to all the seats filled with Eureka citizens eager to hear about the new school before they toured the classrooms when Maggie would be presenting hers. He didn't know

216

if she would be in the audience or in her room waiting for the tour.

People took their seats and the low roar of hundreds of voices in conversation started to diminish.

After a minute, Board of Education President Dr. Bower stood and went up to the podium on the stage. The audience quieted as he introduced soloist Maurine Smith who sang two songs, receiving enthusiastic applause. Dr. Bower then introduced State Superintendent Ross who thanked the crowd for attending and complimented the people of Eureka for building "a magnificent and thoroughly up-to-date school building." He started his address by insisting more attention be given to the physical well-being of the students in light of twenty-nine percent of Selective service-registered men being rejected because of physical deficiencies.

That physical deficiency comment jabbed Ricky in the stomach and he wished the Superintendent hadn't said that.

How do I look? Ricky wondered. Will everyone notice me as one of those rejected "physically deficient" men of which Superintendent Ross referred? Ricky hoped Maggie wasn't present to hear that and see him up at the podium. However, perhaps the podium could hide his "physically-deficient" look. When Superintendent Ross's address wrapped up, Dr. Bower returned to the podium.

"Thank you, Superintendent Ross for that instructive and very inspiring address. Now, please join me in welcoming Eureka's very own Ricky Austin, spokesman for Mueller Construction." He gestured toward Ricky. "Mr. Austin?"

Ricky stood and went to the podium. Dr. Bower shook Ricky's hand and stepped aside.

Ricky looked at the audience. He had heard it helped to pick one person and speak directly to him or her. And there she was. Maggie was toward the back with her friend, Rose.

"Thank you, Dr. Bower," Ricky began.

"Ladies and gentlemen, fellow Eurekans, on behalf of Mueller Construction, welcome to your new Mulberry Street School. Last year, we lost a great building here known as Eastside School, and we have managed to do the impossible and build you a new school in less than a year. As Superintendent Ross mentioned in his fine address, it's a magnificent building. It is of the Classical Revival style architecture like many schools across the country, but ours is one of the best and most beautiful modern schools in Kansas, as Superintendent Ross mentioned. Thanks to the overwhelming support of you, our citizens, our children have an exciting new schoolhouse with fine facilities, a modern heating system, and beautiful classrooms in which to further their education, and for our wonderful teachers in which to conduct their unmatched successes for those children. Thank you very much, and enjoy the tour."

The audience gave Ricky a robust applause, much to his surprise. He smiled and stepped down to his chair. He glanced at the audience and noticed Maggie leaving with Rose for the gym exit. When appropriate, he would join the tour.

* * *

After the closing of the dedication ceremony, Ricky stepped into the first-floor main hallway. Crowds filtered around him, many congratulating him on his address as they headed for classrooms. A familiar voice behind him caught is attention.

"Ready, Mr. Austin?" Benny said, stepping next to him and placing a hand on his shoulder.

Ricky laughed. "You only have to call me mister on special occasions. Ready? Ready for what?"

"The tour, starting with Maggie's classroom."

"All right then," Ricky said as they started walking. "As long as there're no tricks like at the Royal Café."

"Were you unhappy about that?" Benny asked.

"No, but I was a bit embarrassed, and I think she was uncomfortable. I hope she didn't think I put you guys up to that."

"We saw her walking and offered. Like she said, it was spur of the moment."

"I hope so."

"Come on, let's go."

They went to take the north stairs up to the second floor and joined a line, waiting to go into Maggie's classroom. Benny got in front of Ricky and turned to him. "She's absolutely radiant," he said.

Ricky peeked in at Maggie. "She's beautiful," he said.

When it was their turn to step through the door, Maggie was a few feet back, greeting people.

As they all went into the room, Maggie had a big smile.

"Welcome to eighth grade English," she said. "Please look around and notice the modern lighting, and the new radiators to keep your children warm. Be sure to stop by the boiler room in the lower level where Mr. Martin will show you the modern new heating system. And on my desk, you'll find my lesson plan for this week, showing an example of what we're reading and discussing. I have to say that my students are enjoying the class. Especially since we moved out of the high school attic!"

Maggie stepped back and allowed the visitors to approach with questions.

"I have a question for her," Benny said to Ricky. "Let's go over." They stood with several others behind a man and woman who were discussing curriculum with Maggie. After a couple of minutes, they left. Ricky and Benny stepped forward, and Maggie extended her hands, giving Ricky a particularly warm smile.

"Welcome, gentlemen," she said. "Ricky, I was impressed with your address. I didn't know you were a public speaker."

"Actually," said Ricky, "that was my first time to speak in front of an audience…that is, I mean to say, thank you, Maggie. I was glad for the reception. Your room is inspiring, set up and arranged nicely."

"Why, thank you," she said.

"And you look very nice tonight," he said. "As always."

She blushed a little. "Thank you. As do you."

"I have a question, Miss Stilwell," Benny said. "You mentioned the modern lighting. It certainly is that. Do your lights shine steadily?"

"Mine had some flickering," she said, "but they're better lately."

"That'll improve," Benny said.

"Thank you," she said, smiling. "I'm looking forward to brighter days."

"Yes," Benny said. "Let Mr. Martin know if you have any problems."

Ricky smiled. He understood Maggie's comment.

May 22, 1918

Maggie

A few weeks later, Frank H. Brooks was having a sale, and Maggie found she needed an outfit for the coming warmer weather. Best to take advantage of that, with everything getting more expensive these days. She headed down the porch steps of the Oxford in the early afternoon and strolled down Main Street. When she passed Ricky's rooming house, she thought of him sitting there in the mornings and smiled. One of these days, she would stop, and go up to say hello.

There was Rose up ahead walking toward her, smiling herself. She must have noticed Maggie's expression.

When they met, Rose said, "You must have news."

"No, I always feel happy when I walk by his place. I'm trying to figure out how to approach him, but I'm reluctant to. Is it proper for me to?"

"He's more reluctant than you, but don't read anything into that. Are you ready for the sale?"

Maggie shrugged. "I think so. I'm not an avid shopper like some."

Then I'll see you there and help you," said Rose.

"Wonderful," Maggie said, "I need to stop by the bank first." She looked up at the billowing clouds. "I'm glad I brought an umbrella."

"Me, too," said Rose. "All right. See you at Brooks."

Rose went on her way, and Maggie continued on toward the corner of Third and Main. The diagonal corner of the ornate building with the large embedded stone letters "BANK" at the top dominated that corner, rivaled by the Greenwood Hotel which dominated its corner across the intersection.

She reached Citizens National Bank and entered the lobby. Paneled wood abounded and columns seemed to exaggerate the height of the ceiling. She headed toward a cage window under the "Savings Department" sign.

A teller greeted her through the bars. "Hello, Miss Stilwell," he said.

She went to the wooden counter and acknowledged him. "I'd like to withdraw eight dollars and with two of the dollars, I'd like to buy eight twenty-five-cent War thrift stamps."

"Oh, yes," the teller said, getting into a drawer. "Do you have a card started?"

"No, this is my first purchase."

He unfolded a card on the counter. "These sixteen squares are where you can affix the thrift stamps. I'll attach your first eight if you'd like." He set the card's envelope next to it. "Please fill in your name and address here. And congratulations on helping the war effort. Every stamp sold shortens the duration. The bottom explains the value in 1923."

"Thank you," she said, looking at the card. She felt good knowing she was helping. She placed the card and envelope into her bag and walked through the lobby out to the sidewalk. The Frank H. Brooks store was about a block and a half away.

She started down Main Street, and when she entered the store, the smell of new clothes greeted her. Shoppers had crowded into the store, taking advantage of the sale. After browsing a while, she ran into Rose.

"Oh!" said Rose, a dress draped across her arm. "I wanted to show you—"

"Is that intended for me?" Maggie asked.

Rose held the dress up to Maggie. "Will you try it on? I know the material's a bit revealing, but it's lightweight and comfortable, especially during summer."

"I know I tend to be modest. As a teacher, I try to present a proper appearance."

"This isn't for school. It's a summer outfit."

Maggie ran her fingers along the flowing material. "And what if some of my students happen to be out and see me in this?"

"What if *Ricky* sees you in this?" Rose said, winking. "It's a perfectly appropriate dress." She handed the dress to her. "Try it on." She led her to the dressing room.

After consideration, Maggie bought the dress, and they left the store, and started down the sidewalk.

"The sun feels nice today," said Rose, "but it'll only be a few weeks before it's overbearing. Good thing you got that dress."

Having some cash left after her purchase, Maggie led Rose to Mac's Newsstand store when they reached Second and Main Streets where two early-teen kids stood in front of the store trading candy. Maggie and Rose went in and browsed some magazines while Mac arranged items on the counter.

He reached under the counter. "We got a couple of new books in, Maggie. I saved one back for you."

"Thank you, Mac," Maggie said. "I'll have some time to read now with the school year over."

He set an Edgar Rice Burroughs book onto the counter.

Maggie picked the book up and flipped through it. "Just the thing for a few days break," she said.

"I think so, too," he said. "How are things at the new school?"

"Going well, thank you, we love it," she said as she paid for the book.

"Are you going to be busy?" Rose asked her.

"We have Commencement this Friday," said Maggie.

Mac put Maggie's book into a bag. "Are they holding it up at the Princess Theatre?" he asked.

"Yes," she said, "my students will be there."

She thanked him, took her bag, and went to the door with Rose.

"Always nice to see you ladies," Mac said while Maggie and Rose headed out to the sidewalk.

"Oh, there goes the sun," said Rose. "Occasional showers are forecast. I'll head on now. You probably want to get home, too." Rose went on her way.

Maggie walked briskly down the sidewalk. The drifting clouds were getting darker. She considered getting her umbrella ready.

She reached Third Street and felt sprinkles. When she crossed the street, she noticed there were no longer benches sheltered next to the Greenwood Hotel with the current phase of construction, so she crossed Main and went to the gazebo. The rain picked up when she got there. She was in no hurry to go on so she got out her book to read.

She started getting engrossed in the book as the rain picked up and heavier rain battered the gazebo's roof. She huddled on the bench to ward off the slight chill in the misty breeze. It was eighty degrees out before so she hadn't expected a chill, even with some rain.

Splashing footsteps came from the courthouse grounds sidewalk. She turned to look at a soaking wet man dashing toward the gazebo.

"Ricky! come in and try to dry off."

"Thank you, Maggie," he said, sitting across from her, pressing his hair down, dripping.

"Where've you just been?" she asked.

"I have the day off, and I was in the courthouse looking around. The stairs are magnificent. They start really wide on the main floor, leading up from the lobby to a large landing where two more sets of stairs ascend from there to a walkway with banister around the perimeter of the upper part of the large lobby walls."

"Sounds fascinating," she said. "I've only been there for business and have neglected to appreciate the design of it."

"You should consider touring it," he said.

"I'll do that."

The rain tapered off and she put her book away and stood.

He stood and aimed his umbrella down.

They stood a couple of feet apart, facing each other.

"It's nice to see you, Maggie," he said, turning toward the steps.

"And you, Ricky," she said. *Are you going to kiss me?* she thought, then, "Say, Ricky?"

He stopped and turned around. "Yes?"

"No, it's nothing. I'm sorry. Have a good day."

"You too, Maggie," he said as he left.

June 29, 1918

Gerald

I notice someone drive up in a truck outside and pull into the recessed area out front along Mulberry Street. Mr. Martin gets out and rushes through the rain into the building.

"First rain since late May and I have to haul these in through it," he mutters as he hurries in from the front entrance lugging a batch of framed pictures within a portfolio. He sets the portfolio against a wall, and then rushes back to his truck and grabs the other portfolio to lug back in.

Catching his breath, he takes off his coat and hangs it on the stairway's handrail knob.

After a few minutes, he has the portfolios upstairs at the end of the second-floor main hallway on the floor opened unfolded across the floor. I continue south down the wide hallway and go by the history classroom. It looks like he already has the hangers or nails up. He lifts a framed portrait and mounts it.

The rain that pounds against windows roars throughout the building as Mr. Martin hangs more of the portraits around this end of the hall. I tampered with the Julia Gould portrait before to get Ricky's attention.

On the end wall now hangs a portrait of "Miss Mary Service, Principal, Eastside Grade School and Greenwood County Superintendent, 1914–1917." It's a bit crooked and I go to straighten it.

Mr. Martin goes to the wall across from the first and hangs the rest of the portraits then stands back in the middle to look at all of them.

It looks to Mr. Martin that the portrait of Miss Service straightens itself.

He gets goosebumps and steps backward from the portraits.

"Not again," he mumbles, "Somebody playing tricks on me still."

The lightning strikes continue, flashing around the hallways. I like the effect, although I'm not sure Mr. Martin does. For now, I decide to browse the portraits more thoroughly. Some of those teachers are teaching at other schools now, Westside School over on Walnut Street, and the high school. Some have retired, but all seem to have a connection with this location. I wonder how many students they've all taught. I recall Ricky asking that question, a good question.

Mr. Martin is at the north end of the hall now. He looks toward me and runs down the north stairs. A minute later, his truck pulls away from the school building.

I'm alone at last. I'll leave the portraits alone for now.

August 24, 1918

Rose, Doris & Abby

Rose took a seat by herself at one of the fancy linen-draped tables in the Ladies Parlor at the Royal Café where she would meet Maggie for lunch. Two acquaintances, Abby and Doris at a nearby table carried on a conversation Rose couldn't avoid overhearing. She glanced at them periodically.

Doris took a bite from her sandwich and reached across the table to tap the back of Abby's hand. "Why don't they get together?" she asked in a hushed tone.

Abby nodded. "They're both shy."

"They'll never get together like that," Doris said. She snickered. "Unless they've secretly shared a bed."

Abby shrugged. "Who knows? They're two peas in a pod. Wishing good luck for them." She wore a four-leaf clover pendant on a chain around her neck and pulled it to her lips.

Doris took a bite of soup then said, "Maybe if she's seen with a nice gentleman, he'd move."

"A couple come to mind," said Abby.

"Who? That George Fielding fellow?"

Abby shook her head. "Married."

"Benny Hodges then?" suggested Doris.

"No. He and Ricky are friends."

Abby shook her head. "Being seen with someone probably won't do it."

"Then what?" Doris said "New outfits?"

"She usually looks nice," Abby said.

"I mean something that'll turn heads, especially Ricky's."

"Is he observant enough to notice?" Abby said.

"He'd notice her if she wore something revealing," Doris said.

"Maggie? How revealing do you mean?"

"Well," Doris said. "Like that skirt pattern for 1919 that I showed you in *Vogue*, the one that comes up to here." She tapped her upper shin area.

"Every man in town will be staring at that," Abby said. "Maggie would never wear something like that. She doesn't like that much attention. Maybe one of the mid-calf skirts that they're all talking about for next spring."

"Maybe. Sometimes I think she just likes to be by herself," Doris said. "Not very much fun, that girl."

Rose had had enough, got up, and went to their table.

Doris and Abby looked up.

"Why hello, Rosie," Doris said. "Would you like to join us?"

"Yes, thank you," said Rose as she took a seat at the table. "Say, ladies, I didn't mean to eavesdrop, but you should be nicer what you say about Maggie."

"You're right, of course," said Abby. "We should be careful that people don't notice us talking about her."

"Except for you overhearing us, Rose," Doris said, "I'm sure we've kept these things to ourselves."

* * *

Later.

"Why did you bring me here?" Abby asked as she and Doris walked along Mulberry Street toward the school. "I thought we were just out for a walk."

"You won't get over your superstitious obsession if you don't face up to it," Doris said.

"Here?"

"There's been talk about strange happenings here and I assume you've heard about them."

Abby rubbed the clover leaf pendant between her fingers. "I have, but I don't have an obsession. I'm just cautious, that's all."

"Of course you are. Look at you cuddling that clover leaf as if it's got some hold on you."

"I've had this since grade school."

Doris laughed.

"I can tell you some stories," Abby said.

"I'll bet you can. I'm going to take that silly thing from you before we go in."

Abby clenched it. "No."

They continued along the sidewalk toward the front of Mulberry School.

Abby kept a tight grip on the pendant as they turned onto the front sidewalk that led up to the school entrance. "We're actually going in?" she asked.

"Yes we are," Doris said, pointing to a Model T parked along the street. "Mr. Martin's working today so the building should be open."

Abby looked up at the tall windows above the double doors as they approached the entrance. When they reached it, Doris opened one of the doors and they went in.

"Come on, let's go," Doris said, taking Abby's arm.

"Where?"

"Around the halls."

Doris led Abby to the stairway and up to the second floor.

They went through one of the gallery entrances above the gym and went in.

Doris pointed down to the dark gym. "We should go down there and stay for a while in the gloom," she said.

"What for?"

"To wait for anything strange to happen."

A knock from below startled them.

"Mr. Martin," Doris said.

Abby saw movement in the dark. "Did you see that?"

"As I just said, Mr. Martin."

"Then why don't we ask him if he's noticed anything strange?"

Doris shook her head. "He hasn't."

"How do you know?" Abby asked, looking down around the dark expanse.

"Because nothing strange has happened. Come on." Doris led Abby back out to the hallway, strolled around past Maggie's class, and walked down the north side hallway past Mr. Fielding's math class. They went to the far stairway at the northeast corner. When they reached it, Doris gripped the wood handrail and started to step down, but lurched forward as her hand slipped on the rail. She caught herself and Abby helped her back up to the top.

"Too much oil on there," Doris said, shaking her hand.

"Mr. Martin's doing something with it," said Abby. "He's not expecting anyone here today."

"That's right. I should have been careful. Let's go back to the main hallway."

They went back to stroll around the wide hallway and went to the south end toward the portraits.

"Who are these people?" asked Abby.

"Teachers. All of them taught at Eastside School at some time before it burned."

"Are they...still alive?"

"Yes they are. A couple are even teaching here and a few are now at Westside and other schools."

"That's nice to have their portraits on display," Abby said.

"Now you can stay and read all about them," Doris said.

Abby looked around. "What do you mean? You're going to leave me alone here?"

Doris nodded. You're going to spend a little time here by yourself and see there's nothing strange about being alone in this building. Don't worry, these teachers will keep you company."

"Where are you going?" asked Abby.

"Around the school," Doris said. "I missed the dedication in March." She winked and walked away.

"Don't be too long," Abby mumbled.

Doris went on.

Abby kept hold of her clover leaf and went to the first portrait to read about Miss Gould. She tried not to pay attention to the feeling that the portraits were watching her, took a deep breath, and went along the wall to read the captions about the other portraits. Miss Mary Service's portrait was interesting: A teacher, a principal, and superintendent. Abby stepped away from it and stood in the middle of the hallway.

The quiet surrounded her.

"You're all very accomplished," she said aloud, listening to the echo. "I don't know that I could do what you do. Maybe I could, but it takes someone special like each of you to teach young people who'll be leaders of tomorrow. I hope they all grow to appreciate you one day."

She stopped talking and waited for the slight echo to fade.

Pacing around a little, she started talking again. "Why is Doris leaving me alone like this? It's all right I guess." She looked around at the portraits and smiled. "Aren't I doing fine, ladies?"

Knocking sounds from the gym gallery entrance gave her a start. She crept over and peeked in. All was still except for slight knocks and thumps out in the darkness. It was unnerving so she stepped back to the hallway.

* * *

After a while, Doris strolled around the first-floor north hallway, went past the gym entrance near the stage and decided to go in. There was enough light to make her way along the stage. A draft wafted through the gym and gave her chills. She wrapped her arms around herself and walked a little. When she heard the sound of clothing brushing against the edge of the stage, she went to the exit to the south hall. Her back arched forward instinctively as she hurried to get to the exit as fast as possible. At the door, a puff of air from behind sent her hair flying and she jumped into the hallway. Walking along the hall, she went past the restrooms. For a split-second, she heard a shower noise and turned around to hurry to the southeast stairway and started up the stairs. When she reached the second-floor hall, she stopped by the library and for a second heard a voice from there. She looked ahead and noticed the portraits area at the far end of the dim hall where Abby waited. Doris crept toward there as quietly as she could, trying not to panic.

When she reached the portraits, Abby wasn't there. She looked around at Miss Gould and nearby portraits. Some light scraping on the south wall grabbed her attention.

Miss Service's portrait was swinging back and forth. Doris ran out to the middle of the main hallway to near the stairway and gasped. She heard a tap where the north hall joined the main hallway near Maggie's and Mr. Fielding's classrooms.

A dozen pinpoint dots in random formation emerged from the north hallway and floated across the main hallway, and hovered outside Maggie's door.

Doris tried to scream but couldn't. She ran down the stairs.

Abby was down there alone by the front doors staring at Doris with a blank expression.

Doris gasped "Abby!"

"I saw something," Abby whispered.

"Let's go!" Doris said.

She lunged at Abby, grabbed her hand, and pulled her outside.

Outside on the steps, Doris led Abby to the curb and pointed down at the Model T parked on the street.

"That's not Mr. Martin's car," she said. "He's not here."

September 9, 1918

Annie

On this early morning, Annie looked through a stack of old copies of *The Eureka Herald* and *Democratic Messenger* weekly newspapers for an article, something she remembered reading the year before. After a while, she found it. "Eureka!" she said.

An article in the June 14, 1917 *Messenger* said: "Work commenced on the new grade school Monday morning. The work will be pushed as rapidly as possible. It is hoped to have the building ready for occupancy by January 1st."

"Well," she muttered, "no wonder they're still fixing things."

She put the newspapers away and started to get ready for the first day of school. A little later, kids started entering the building. Some commotion and laughter in the hallway drew her to the door. A primary school boy ran past her.

Annie grabbed his arm. "What's the matter with you, young man!" she said, scolding. "You walk straight to your class now."

The boy went down the hall swinging his arms.

Back in the library, Annie checked over everything. She went to the north shelves to the bookcases and straightened some books. It mostly looked fine except for a book in the wrong place. She reached for the book and *something* tripped her, sending her stumbling a few feet back from the bookshelf.

The long bulletin board from above the bookcase crashed to the floor in front of her.

Dazed, she sat up.

Two teachers rushed in. "Are you all right?" asked one.

The other offered her hand and helped Annie up.

"Oh my goodness!" said Annie. "Phew! I just tripped over something."

"If you hadn't fallen, that bulletin board could have hurt you."

October 11, 1918

Maggie

With gathering places now closed until the 21st due to the influenza epidemic, Maggie decided to go up to the school and do some organizing in her classroom and work on lesson plans. As she walked up the small hill amid early fall greens and yellows of the foliage above, some yellow leaves floated down.

She reached Mulberry Street and strolled toward the school enjoying the seventy-degree weather and the light fog of which the rain the day before was responsible. She could see the outline of Mr. Martin's old pickup truck parked along Second Street on the south side of the school grounds. She continued on to the front doors. Once inside, she climbed the stairway and went toward her classroom.

"Well," she said aloud, "Ricky, what am I going to do with you? Would it be too forward of me to approach you and settle this friendship once and for all? I'm not sure. These *are* modern times. It's almost the 1920s after all. We women are getting closer to the Vote. The House passed the Amendment. In light of that, we women are getting more freedoms. Although we've got a ways to go."

As usual when she stopped talking, her voice echoes faded and quiet returned except for knocking about noises around the building by Mr. Martin. She reached her classroom, went in, using a handkerchief on the door handle.

She went to her desk and set her purse next to a small stack of books and her globe. Mr. Martin was out making rounds, so she got up to get ready for him to take care of anything needed in her room. She walked up and down the aisles between the desks and went to the bookshelves on the back wall and started straightening books. She paced around the room a little and went to the windows to raise one a bit and allow in the breeze. Back at the bookshelves, she knelt and arranged some bottom shelf books.

Mr. Martin was working in a nearby classroom. She got up and left the room to go for a short walk down the hall and looked at the portraits for a bit. When she returned, Mr. Martin was already in the classroom emptying the waste basket.

"Hello, Mr. Martin," she said, stepping through her door. "How is everything? Two more weeks, hopefully we'll be open."

"It gives me time to attend to some things without impacting anyone."

He wheeled his cart out and Maggie relished the quiet and imagined her students back in those empty desks, eager to resume studies.

October 31, 1918

Maggie

On a warm, sunny Halloween afternoon, Mr. Gray emerged from the Royal Café holding two dishes of ice cream and handed them to Maggie and Rose. "You may take these up to the gazebo and enjoy," he said.

They thanked him and hurried toward the courthouse grounds to settle into the gazebo before the ice cream melted.

"Wait, there's a young couple in the gazebo," said Rose. "Let's not bother them."

Maggie and Rose went and sat on the courthouse steps.

"I hate how this epidemic has changed so many things this year what with restaurants and so many places having to close," said Maggie, taking a bite of ice cream. "Not to mention the poor souls who've lost their lives right here in Eureka, as well as some of our brave soldiers. Look at us enjoying ice cream this afternoon when I would normally be at school, teaching today."

"Are you making any progress with Ricky?" asked Rose, tapping Maggie's wrist. "You can tell me."

"I'm thinking of ways."

"I can help you think of things."

"Oh, well," Maggie said, stirring her melting ice cream. "Say, look over at the gazebo."

"They're kissing!" Rose said. "Maybe there ought to be a bell to ring when that happens."

"Except some prefer to keep it private," said Maggie.

"Most of them don't," said Rose.

Rose stood and picked up their dishes. "I'll return these to Mr. Gray," she said, getting ready to head back to the café.

Maggie thanked her and went to the sidewalk. The autumn weather felt nice as she strolled along Main Street.

She turned west along Third Street and left downtown, walking along the tree-lined street. She looked around to see if anyone was near and started talking in a soft voice.

"Well, Ricky, I've decided I'm going to think of ways to get us together, because I think you want that as much as I do. I know of your love of architecture and I had thought of using that somehow to get to you, but I'm mostly ignorant of the subject and doubt I could use it correctly to get your attention. I do have a good appreciation for different architectural styles."

She thought about it as she gazed up at the yellow foliage, and noticed neighborhood kids watching as she kept walking and talking softly.

Sunset came earlier in October so she went back toward downtown. The courthouse was already casting a long shadow in the low sun, the shadow stretching onto the store fronts across Main Street. Maggie stopped and looked up at the ornate courthouse.

"Get ready, Mr. Austin, Miss Stilwell's got an idea and there'll be no escape for you!"

November 11, 1918

Maggie, et al

Armistice Day

Rose came over to the Oxford amid an early gathering of activity outside. Maggie and Mrs. Thrall greeted her. "Isn't it wonderful!" she said.

Maggie and Rose hugged.

George and Nancy Fielding entered the living room. "The war is over! People are assembling for a spur of the moment parade!"

The cheering spread among all of them and they all went to the window to watch where people had formed a line with their cars on North Main Street, excited drivers already honking their horns. More citizens joined the parade from side streets with various noise-making devices.

"Shall we go?" said Maggie. She and the others went to the sidewalk and watched the cars roll past. They were decorated with flags and dragging metal milk cans tied to their back bumpers making a clanking racket, the cars now filled with people cheering along with more marchers who came carrying flags, banging on buckets and tubs as the noise level surged.

Maggie, Rose, George, and Nancy joined the parade toward the back as others emerged from side streets and joined the marchers. Maggie nearly tripped over a metal milk jug. Rose grabbed it and tossed it to Nancy who started banging on it with her fist. Maggie jumped over next to her and hit the bucket as well. A woman behind them had an extra flag and tapped Rose to offer it to her. She took it and continued to contribute to the noise as they roared down Main Street. As they crossed Sixth Street, more revelers joined them, some with cow bells and anything that made a lot of noise, tin pans to add to the roar of horns, cheering, and clanking.

At Third Street, several men came out of an office in the Crebo building and joined the parade a little ways back.

They continued south along Main, where spectators stood on the sidewalks cheering the parade on with more cheering as revelers walked along the Opera Block, people cheering from upper windows.

When Maggie and her friends reached the bonfire, they found a spot in the gathering semicircle of spectators. The band started playing patriotic songs.

Doris stood across from them in the semicircle. She waved toward Maggie and friends. Maggie started to return the wave, then Rose looked behind them and noticed Abby waving back at Doris. "Hello, Abby," she said.

"Where are George and Nancy?" Maggie shouted.

"Right behind you," Nancy shouted.

Maggie turned around and they were there with Ricky.

George threw his arms up. "Isn't it fabulous?"

"It is indeed," said Ricky.

Ricky went with Maggie and friends as they joined the revelers who started back north on Main.

December 23, 1918

Ricky

Ricky sat at the small desk in his somewhat spartan room at the Main Street Rooming House and finished wrapping a gift.

"I hope she likes this," he muttered. "I don't know if it's good, but hopefully it's the thought that counts."

He went to sit on his bed and pulled on his snow boots then grabbed his heavy coat, scarf, and gloves from the small closet. All set, he went to open his door to the hallway. The owner had kindly left a shovel for him there as he had requested in anticipation of the heavy snow already piling up out on Main Street. If he cleared some of the snow now and more accumulated in the afternoon, then he'd just go back out again. Best to keep things safe.

He grabbed the shovel and went down to the living room.

The owner met him. "You go after I do the steps," the owner said.

Ricky waited then took the shovel onto the porch and went to the front sidewalk. He would finish that after a while. He trudged north and when he reached the Oxford, he started shoveling the porch steps. He had seen their handyman shoveling before. As that man was up in years, Ricky didn't like seeing him exerting himself in the bitter cold. He hoped taking the initiative to shovel the steps and sidewalk for this boarding home wasn't an assertion to display his manhood by usurping their handyman's task. He knew Benny would say that's a strange way for a man to think. But Benny had been chiding Ricky ever since they met and it was Benny's way of trying to help.

A car's spinning tires caught his attention, someone in a Buick was trying to make it through the deeper snow at Sixth and Main, the snow halfway up its wheels.

Ricky set the shovel down and went to join another person who had just gotten out of the car to push on the back bumper and they started heaving the car forward. They pushed it out of the deeper snow and it regained some traction. The other person hurried around and climbed back into the car after offering thanks. Ricky waved and walked back across the street. As he was making his way toward the side of the snowy street, another car started skidding toward him. He tried to get out of the way, but slipped the wrong way toward the car's path. Just as he feared getting hit, something pushed him out of the way, knocking him to the street away from the sliding car as it skidded around him.

He stood, caught his breath, and started to make his way to the Oxford's front sidewalk where he continued shoveling.

After a few more minutes, the front walk was clear for now; he went to check the porch steps and shoveled them once more to be sure.

Mrs. Thrall leaned out the door. "Is that you, Mr. Austin?" she asked.

"Yes, ma'am," he said, catching his breath. "I believe I'm done for now." She pulled the door open a little, and he started to turn to walk away.

"Don't you dare leave!" she shouted. "Get yourself in here by the warm fire."

He smiled and nodded, climbing the steps, setting the shovel aside, and Mrs. Thrall brought him in.

As they stepped into the living room, the women sitting there, including Maggie, greeted him. Mrs. Thrall helped him with his coat, scarf and gloves, then took his arm and led him to one of the wingback chairs next to the fireplace.

"Oh, that's nice," he said holding his palms toward the roaring fire.

"We have hot tea or coffee or hot chocolate made," said Mrs. Thrall. "What would you like?"

"Hot chocolate would be fabulous," he said.

She nodded at Maggie. "Would you bring our guest a nice hot chocolate?"

Maggie stood, smiled at Ricky, and wiggled her fingers discretely as she left for the kitchen.

Ricky relished the warmth and admired the Christmas tree in the bay window behind the sofa; he stood as Maggie returned to the living room. She placed the cup onto a side table next to him. "Here you are. Please sit and relax." She went to the other wingback chair also by the fireplace.

After a while, Hazel got up and left the living room. She returned down the stairs and set a box of cards on the coffee table in front of the sofa.

"Would anyone like to play Logomachy?" she said as she sat on the sofa.

Mrs. Thrall came in from the kitchen. "I should like to join you all," she said.

"Of course," said Hazel. "I was getting ready to ask if everyone knows how to play Logomachy?"

"I haven't played it but would like to learn," said Mrs. Thrall.

"All right. Anyone else?" asked Hazel. "Mr. Austin? Maggie? Norma?"

"We played this when Abe was alive," Norma said. "He used to spell out insults to other players, the onery old coot."

"I've played it as well," said Maggie.

"Yes," said Ricky, "I used to play Logomachy with my cousin Clyde when I lived in El Dorado."

"Well," Hazel said to Mrs. Thrall. "It's a word game played with these cards." She put her hand on the card deck. "First, we shuffle the deck and deal them out. Each card has a letter on it. We go around and place our cards on the table to spell words. If your card adds to the spelling of a word, you score."

"That sounds fun," said Mrs. Thrall.

They played for a couple of hours. Norma ended her last turn completing the word "friends."

"Oh that's a nice word," said Maggie. She ended her last turn completing the word "are."

Ricky ended his turn completing the word, "appreciated."

"I think the cards are expressing all our feelings for you, Mr. Austin," said Hazel.

"Unquestionably," said Maggie. "That was so kind of you today."

Ricky nodded and smiled at her.

"Mr. MacGregor thanks you as well," said Mrs. Thrall.

Ricky stood and took his coat and scarf from the coat rack. "Thank you all for an enjoyable afternoon," he said, which was met with a chorus of 'yesses'.

Before he started to leave, he reached into his pocket and handed a small present to Maggie. "This is for you. Merry Christmas."

"Thank you," she said. "I didn't get you anything."

"Think nothing of it," he said as she went and placed it under the tree.

* * *

On Christmas Day, Maggie and her housemates exchanged gifts. She later went up to her room, sat on the edge of her bed, and opened the small present from Ricky. The enclosed note said:

Dear Maggie, This card holder is special to me; I'd like you to have it. —Fondly, Ricky."

Maggie clutched it and held it to her lips. "Thank you, Ricky."

January 3, 1919

Gerald

Ol' Rick-boy did all right around Christmastime. He still needs to work on presenting himself better, be more assertive. I know that if he could sense my thoughts, he'd say that's not his way, but he needs to work on it.

And the ol' card holder. Nice to see it pop up again. He figured that right both times. It was good of him to shovel the walk and porch and save Mr. MacGregor from the task.

But I hope he starts looking out for himself better. I don't want to keep following him around, saving him from his own clumsiness.

I don't know what else to think about it. I need to take a break from walking up and down the main hallway, so I step into Principal Nibert's office to snoop around. After a while, I look out his office window at the bitter cold day outside. Still some snow around; it'll probably linger for a while. Even in my state of being, I look forward to spring with its flowers and sprouting leaves, A start over for the plant and animal world.

I soon bore of snooping around in here and slide through the wall into the main hallway. Mr. Martin's here today, having braved the cold to get here in his old pickup. I heard him on this floor earlier, but I think he's in the basement now. I'd like to have some fun with him as he reacts well to my manifestations. Rather than be scared, he just gets mad and that's much more fun. Then

248

again, I shouldn't underestimate the joy of a good scare. The one called Doris is fun. Oozing with an over-abundance of self-confidence, that know-it-all puts on a good show. But I'm trying to be good, although after saving Ricky *twice* and the librarian once from harm, I'm entitled to a little recreation, aren't I?

Let's see—where is Mr. Martin? I'm already feeling guilty, but I'm looking for him anyway. I wish I had an audible voice. It'd be fun to yell "Booooooo" and let that echo through the halls, but I suppose I should stick with lesser "crimes" so I don't cause him to quit. As a wise one once said, "A dog doesn't bite the hand that feeds it."

All right, I hear something going on in the basement, so Mr. Martin is down there. I want to find out what he's up to, so I go down the southeast stairway.

The door to the boiler room is open and he's in there working. I look in, and he's on the floor doing something with the plumbing under the boiler. He reaches for a wrench on the floor behind him and starts banging on the pipe. He mumbles something about why he was having to do this with a new boiler and rolls onto his back then takes the wrench and strikes something in the twisting pipes under the boiler. Whatever he's trying to do, he's unsuccessful and sets the wrench down, gets on his side to face the boiler as he reaches under it to take hold of a valve then reaches out with his other hand for the wrench.

The wrench slides an inch away. He grabs for it and it slides a couple more inches.

"What!" he shouts, sitting up and the wrench slides across the concrete out of reach.

He jumps up and watches the tools put themselves away. As he backs away toward the hallway, the valve he was trying to manipulate gushes hot water, spraying the floor where he was lying.

He's all right. Tricking him was fun and I saved him from being scalded.

* * *

Now that I've done my good deed for today and have completed my daily snooping, I'm going out for a while. Let's see. How about downtown? Haven't been there for a few days.

Downtown isn't very busy, probably because of the harsh cold with that pleasant little breeze that helps make it so miserable to people. As I go along toward downtown, I see Maggie turn from Main and walk down West Third street. Halfway down the block, a breeze catches her scarf, causing it to sail away. She tries to lunge for it, but can't grab it and it flies away. She reaches West 3rd Street Grocery and goes in. I can't go after the scarf for her until it settles to the ground so I follow her into the small store, past a rack with magazines and books. She's greeted by Mr. Mack, who stands behind the wooden checkout counter.

"Hello, Miss Stilwell," he says. "It's a blustery day, isn't it?"

"Hello, Mr. Mack," she says, pulling her coat around. "It sure is. And not a good day to lose one's scarf."

"Breeze catch it?" He leans down to reach under the counter and pulls out a spare scarf. "Take this one for your walk home. It probably won't match your outfit, but it'll keep you warm."

"Thank you so much," she says.

"You'll need one."

"Hopefully I'll find mine before school starts back up after the holidays."

"Anything I can help you with?" he says.

She points up to the woven baskets hanging high above the produce area along the wall. "I'd like one of those baskets with the horizontal stripes around the side."

"I thought you would," he says, smiling as he steps out from behind the counter, grabs a step ladder, and climbs up. "Which one?" he says.

"One of those two in the middle," she says.

He reaches for one and brings it down to her. "Going on a picnic?" he says, laughing.

She smiles. "Maybe later. I've been eyeing this for weeks." She sets it on the counter.

"Anything else?" he asks.

She eyes a pastry in a display case. "Now that's why I braved the cold. I've got a craving for—that one," she says, pointing to it.

He goes to the glass case, retrieves the one she indicates, and takes it to the counter.

They finish up and Maggie prepares to leave.

I realize I've been lax about something and slip outside to the sidewalk as she exits the store. I spot her scarf where it has sailed across the street to the courthouse grounds. A stronger breeze picks it up and carries it over to the Greenwood Hotel where it gets caught on some scaffolding. I hurry over, climb up, and grab it. I know just where to take it. I wave it to mimic it sailing in the wind and carry it down to the sidewalk to where I will pull it across Third Street toward the Crebo Building to the office door marked "Temporary Offices of Mueller Construction." I can't take it inside with the door closed so I'll wait.

As it's close to lunch time, I don't have to wait for long. Ricky emerges from the office with Mr. Mueller and they appear to be headed toward Main Street, so I "fly" the scarf across Third and drape it around Ricky's shoulders.

"Look," Ricky says to Mueller, bringing it across his nose.

"Your lucky day," Mueller says.

"I can't keep it, because I think I know who it belongs to."

"As I said, 'your lucky day'."

"Aw, cut it out," Ricky says.

Their laughter fades as they walk to Main Street.

I wait as they go to Eureka Cafeteria for lunch, not far from West 3rd Street Grocery.

So I wait again for them to emerge from the restaurant. After they do, Mueller heads back to the office, and Ricky takes the scarf up to the Oxford.

January 25, 1919

Maggie, et al

The soft roar of dozens of people greeted Maggie and Rose when they entered the school. They went to the gym and paid the fifteen-cent admission then joined a crowd viewing over one hundred reproductions of masterworks of art that were on display.

Maggie gazed around. "Aren't these wonderful?" she said.

"Magnificent."

George Fielding approached. "Good afternoon, ladies," he said. "Great day for a fundraiser, isn't it? I think the spring-like weather brought people out. By the way, Maggie, I ran into Ricky downtown today and he said he's coming to the exhibit."

Annie joined them. "Hello, Maggie, Rose, George," she said. "How are you all doing? You're looking well, Maggie."

They acknowledged her.

"Well," said Annie, "Here comes Louise Pangborn."

"Oh, dear," said Maggie.

Louise stepped up to them. "Hello, everyone! Aren't these paintings marvelous?"

"They're very close matches to the originals," said Maggie.

"Aren't they, though?" Louise said.

"There's a fine art book in the library with full-color pictures of most of these," said Maggie.

"Well, I've seen most of these in person," Louise said, "in the Louvre." She smiled and touched Rose's shoulder with her fingertips. "That's in Paris, France."

"Yes, I've been there, too," said Rose.

"Of course you have," said Louise. "I'm sure John took you; God rest his soul. How are you getting along?"

"Better without him."

"Oh." Louise turned to Maggie.

Uh oh, Maggie thought.

Louise reached over and tapped her fingertips on Maggie's arm. "And how are you doing with gentleman prospects?"

Annie stood behind Louise and made a kissy face.

Maggie almost burst out laughing.

"Keep at it, dear," said Louise. "You're good enough for many men."

Annie nodded and smiled in a mocking gesture.

"All right," Louise said, turning to George. "And Mr. Fielding, you're as handsome as ever. Out without your wedding ring, I see?"

"Mrs. Fielding had him leave it at home so he can flirt with the ladies," said Annie.

George smiled, embarrassed. "Mrs. Fielding will be along shortly. My ring's at the jeweler being repaired."

"Oh, now," said Louise. "Well, you all enjoy the art show." She turned and left.

"What a card." said Annie, laughing.

Maggie smiled. "Let's go view some reproductions."

They looked around the perimeter of the gym to decide where to start. Several teachers had gathered around some displays in front of the stage.

"Let's go," said Annie.

Maggie looked around first, but didn't see Ricky.

They reached those displays; two teachers stood talking next to a couple of paintings and Ruby Francis, the art teacher, was explaining something about one of the paintings.

Ruby gestured to a landscape scene and turned to Maggie. "Look at this one by Claude Monet, *Wild Poppies Near Argenteuil*. Doesn't that look like our countryside around Eureka?"

Maggie leaned toward it and gazed at the scene of reddish-orange poppies on a grassy hillside with a few trees on the hilltop and background, and with a woman carrying an umbrella accompanying a girl with flowers.

"Why yes," said Maggie. "It does!" She turned to Rose and Annie. "Do you like the somewhat new impressionism style?"

"It's all right," said Rose.

"Sometimes it's obvious if you just look carefully," said Annie.

Ricky came up to them. "May I join you all?"

"Yes, of course," they all said.

Maggie stepped aside to give Ricky some room.

She peered at another painting near the Monet work, one of a woman in a blue and white dress assisting a young person seated at a desk holding a page of a book while the woman tapped it with a pointing object. "Oh, what's that work called?" Maggie asked.

Ruby smiled. "It's *The Teacher* by Jean Baptiste Simeon."

"When was it painted?"

"1740. Notice the style difference between it and that one to the right, *The Reluctant Courtship* by Henry Andrews, which was painted over a hundred years later. Maybe it's just me, but I think placement of these works is important. I didn't place *The Teacher* next to the Henry Andrews work."

Maggie stepped back and gazed at the two paintings side by side. "Very interesting placement," she said.

"Certainly is," said Ricky.

February 1, 1919

Maggie

On an unusual fifty-eight-degree February afternoon, Maggie went down the Oxford's porch steps and paused for a moment to see how warm it felt. Her wool skirt and matching jacket were just right for this and for something else. Her laced-up shoes with round toes and lower wedge heels were quite comfortable for walking. So she went to the sidewalk and started walking down along Main Street. When she reached Ricky's rooming house, she slowed to a gradual stroll, and be as that it may, the nice weather had drawn him out to sit on the porch with Benny where they were talking and relaxing so she didn't have to keep watch and try later. She stopped and waved at Ricky with wiggling fingers and a smile.

He returned the smile and stood. "Nice day for a walk, isn't it, Miss Stilwell?" he said.

"It certainly is," she said. "Perhaps you'd like to join me?"

"I'd be honored," he said, stepping down from the porch to join her.

As they started walking, Ricky looked around. "Well," he said. "Where would you like to go?"

"I have always been impressed with many of the building styles around town, on Main Street and elsewhere."

"Why, I would love to walk around with you and point out what I know," he said, smiling. "What places do you have in mind?" he asked. "I'll walk with you to those places and I won't bore you by rattling through a list of styles."

"You won't bore me with that. I want to know," she said. "Let's go up to the Carnegie Library."

They headed north to the library and stood in front of it.

"Now, he said, "notice the large brick columns on either side of the steps and the stone beams around the windows and the front doors. Those are characteristic of Classical Revival style, getting popular since the turn of the century. I believe there are more buildings of that style planned in Eureka."

"A little less ornate than some others."

"Certainly is." He looked down Main Street. "Where to?"

"Let's go down to Second and Main."

"All right."

They started walking a ways and reached Third Street.

"Let's cross Main and walk on that side."

They stood on the curb, and Maggie felt Ricky's hand slip into hers as they stepped off the curb. She clasped it and they went across.

"Well," said Maggie, laughing as they went to the west side of Main Street, "I guess we'll give people something to talk about."

"No doubt of that," he said with a chuckle. "Say, there's the courthouse."

"Let's go to some other places first and come back," she said.

"Very well. I believe we were headed to Second and Main.

They crossed Third and continued to Citizens National Bank on the corner.

"What style is this bank building?" she asked.

"Romanesque. Notice the ornate upper design."

When they started to pass Clark Drug Store, Ricky said, "Say, would you like to stop in for an ice cream soda? My treat."

"I'd love to."

They went in and over a dozen patrons turned and stared, most of them smiling, and Maggie went to one of the vacant counter stools. The young woman occupying the one next to it moved over to free one up for Ricky. The attendant took their orders and brought two chocolate sodas in tall glasses.

Neither Maggie nor Ricky was talkative at the moment. Maggie considered that, but it was not for lack of what to say. She was enjoying their time together, and it seemed he was as well.

When they finished, they went out and resumed their walk toward Second Street.

Near the corner, she gestured to the stone-block front Olney Drug building. "What architectural style is that building?" she asked.

"It's Italianate architecture. Built in 1877, a popular style for commercial buildings in the late 1800s. Note the Eureka Bank building next door on the corner with the same Italianate architecture. That's the oldest building downtown, built in 1876. I hope it stays well maintained."

"I hope so, too; it's a beautiful building," she said.

They continued hand in hand across Main Street and followed Second Street east until they reached Elm Street. Maggie led him north toward Third Street to where the First Congregational Church stood on the corner.

"What is this magnificent architecture?" she said, gazing up at the tall bell tower and steeple on the massive stone church.

"It's Romanesque, like Citizens Bank. It's a popular style for churches and banks."

"Beautiful," she said. "Let's walk through a neighborhood or two. How about up by Mulberry School?"

"Of course. Lead the way."

They walked Maggie's usual route along East Third, and when they walked up the hill, Ricky gestured to some of the houses.

"Nice bungalow style houses here," he said.

She looked around. "I love them. I think one would suit me well."

"I can see um—you in one. Many of them are adorned with fine woodwork by craftsmen. It's a newer style, around about twenty-five or thirty years and has grown in popularity."

They reached Mulberry Street and stopped. She pointed to the big house on the northwest corner. "What style is that house?"

"People are calling that Victorian style now, although I think Edwardian might be also be descriptive. Experts differ on that."

"Let's go along the houses across from the school. I walk by them daily when school is in session."

"Yes, of course."

They went by a house with a porch supported by round columns.

"That's what I call a modified foursquare, as it's taller than it is wide. It's a popular style on the East Coast."

"And what is the new Mulberry School?" she asked gesturing to it to their left across the street.

"Classical revival. Very popular with new school buildings."

They walked on toward the corner where a large house with wraparound porch stood.

"This I call Victorian or modified Edwardian," he said. "Notice the octagonal turret with bay windows."

"Well, now, shall we head to the courthouse?" she suggested.

"Yes, let's go."

They turned back toward Third Street, started down the hill toward downtown while Maggie picked up the pace a little.

"The courthouse is beautiful inside and out," he said.

"I've only been inside a few times on business, so I haven't seen much of it" she said.

They walked the several blocks along Third Street to Main and crossed to the courthouse grounds.

Ricky gestured to the massive stone building. "This magnificent building is French Renaissance style architecture. It was designed by John G. Haskell who designed other similar courthouses in Kansas, including the one in Cottonwood Falls. Haskell moved to Kansas when he was aged twenty-five."

"Well then," she said, "interesting age similarity, isn't it?"

"I like to think so."

"Let's go in," she said. "I want to see those stairs you mentioned."

She led him by the hand, and they hurried inside. The stairway was everything he had described that rainy day. She ascended the stairs herself.

"Coming up?" she said.

He walked up the steps and caught up. They went to the upper walkway and he held onto her hand securely when they looked down to the main floor below.

"All right," she said. "you're not comfortable with heights, I can tell. Let's go back to the main floor."

She led him down the stairs and gazed around at the inside ornate Greek columns and the woodwork. He pointed to a couple of doors around the lobby. "Those two lead into the courtroom." He pointed up. "The county jail is up on the third floor."

"I don't need to see that," she said. "Let's head on."

Out front on the stone steps, she said, "Thank you so much for the wonderful tour. I really have enjoyed this afternoon."

"You're quite welcome," he said. "I really enjoyed this afternoon, too."

They walked hand in hand along the diagonal sidewalk toward Main Street.

"Are you ready to head home?" he said as they got closer to Main Street.

"Soon, but tell me the style of that cute gazebo." She pointed toward it.

"Some would call that gingerbread."

"Well, it fits. Show me up close what makes it that style," she said, leading him toward it.

When they reached the steps, Ricky pointed to the decorative work under the eaves. "That's what gives it that description."

Maggie let go of his hand, went up into the gazebo, stood in the middle, and pointed up. "What about this?"

He went up and faced her.

They stood for a moment then dove into each other's arms.

They kissed, locked in an inseparable embrace that neither tried to break for who knows how long.

About a year later, March 13, 1920

Maggie & Ricky

Ricky waited in the gazebo and noticed Maggie rounding the corner across the street next to the hotel. Her expression brightened when she noticed Ricky standing there. She hurried over and caught her breath when she joined him.

"I'm glad we could meet here today," Ricky said.

"How could we not?" she said.

He took her hand. "A year now," he said.

"And about two years since we met at the post office when you stumbled against me," she said. "And it took you a year to get up the nerve to show your intentions to me here, for which I had to take the initiative!"

He shook his head. "I was clear about my feelings."

"No, and I tried to be ladylike and resist, and although I considered being more forward much earlier, but wasn't sure how you would take that."

"I don't think being ladylike should get in the way of one's goals," he said.

"I'm happy to hear that," she said.

"Obviously I wouldn't have had a problem with that."

She reached into her picnic basket. "I could tell," she said.

"I figured."

"Ready to start lunch?" She took out some bread, cheese, and an apple, and broke some bread off, sliced a little cheese, and offered some to him.

They huddled close to each other in the cool weather as they had lunch.

After a while, they relaxed in each other's arms as they sat back, feet stretched out as they watched the Saturday traffic roll by. An occasional driver honked and waved.

Maggie stirred later and sat up. "I want to go by the school for a bit. Would you walk with me?"

"I'd be honored, Miss Stilwell," he said.

They stood, embraced and went to the sidewalk. Walking hand in hand to Third Street, they headed to Mulberry School. Once inside, they went up to her classroom. She unlocked the door, they went in, and Ricky went to look out the window as she gathered some things from her desk. Then she smiled as she turned to see him with his arms out beckoning her to join him.

"The school is two years old now," he said. "How about a kiss to break this room in."

"Ha! Junior High kids? This room has seen more kissing than you can imagine."

"All right. I give up. I know I'm a little naïve."

"A little?" she said as she went to him.

"Well maybe the first adult kiss," he said, embracing her and planting a long kiss.

"I doubt that was the first adult kiss," she said.

"Well, before I embarrass myself into a frenzy, how about you show me around. I'd like to see how you've all settled in."

She took his hand and led him out to the hallway.

"Have you seen what we call our Hall of Portraits?" she said, taking him to the south end of the hall where he immediately noticed Miss Gould's portrait near a small picture of a building.

"Great teacher," he said. "Had her for fourth grade at Eastside when we lived here."

He regarded the other portraits. "In fact, a lot of these teachers taught at Eastside."

"It's a nice display and many of the students find it interesting to learn about the teachers from Eastside." She pointed to a picture of the old schoolhouse at the beginning of the portraits. "They just added this picture. Such a nice old building."

"I remember it well," he said.

"Let me show you the library," Maggie said, starting to go down the south side hall. When they reached the library entrance, she unlocked the door. They stepped in, and Ricky looked around the library shelves lining the wall. A book caught his eye.

"Oh!" he shouted.

"Goodness," she said. "You nearly scared me half to death!"

"I'm sorry, I just noticed this book on the history of architecture. Amazing you have it here. I'm impressed."

"Annie is always vigilant for new titles. She always attends the parent-teacher meetings and researches what the high schools are acquiring."

"Very nice library," he said as they started out to the hallway and walked to the southeast stairway. They went down and when they reached the first-floor landing, Ricky stopped.

"What was that?" he said.

"What was what?"

"That bump from the basement."

"We hear noises like that all the time," she said. "The building's probably settling."

"Settling doesn't sound like that," he said.

Maggie shrugged. "Do you want to go down there?"

"Maybe for a couple of minutes."

In the main hall down there, they walked toward the north end and toward the art room and halted when whistling came from behind them.

"Now that's not normal," said Maggie, whispering.

"That sounded like it came from the boiler room. Is Mr. Martin here?"

"His truck isn't."

Ricky and Maggie both rubbed their arms through their sleeves to calm the goosebumps.

Another clanking noise from behind startled them.

They clasped hands and went to the northeast stairway.

"Are most of these the usual noises?" Ricky asked as they ascended the stairs.

"Hard to say," she said. "Rumors abound."

"I've heard about them."

A knock from the upper stairs discouraged them from going back up to the second floor.

When they reached the main floor, they headed west along the hall, past the gym entrance.

"Now there's a spooky place," said Maggie.

"Then we don't need to go in there," Ricky said, chuckling as they walked along. Then they heard a knock just behind them and hurried to the main hallway and walked toward the middle.

After passing the principal's office, they stopped along the wall opposite the main stairway.

"Does it seem like those thumps chased us here?" he said.

"It sure does."

"Well, Miss Stilwell, may I walk you home?"

"Yes," she said. "I should get to my Saturday tasks and, by the way, I don't expect to be called 'miss' forever."

266

"Nor should you," he said.

"Thank you," she said, smiling.

He nodded. "We'll figure how to remedy that."

"Do you have a suggestion? Or are you too shy?"

"I'm not shy after a good night's sleep," he said.

"Will you sleep well tonight after our scary little walk around the school?"

"It won't matter, because I had a good night's sleep last night."

"Well then," she said.

On that place where the scaffolding had been, Ricky got down on one knee.

Early January 2003

Epilogue

Gerald

Ricky and Maggie would both have been around 110 years old by now and they had long, happy lives together.

Now I stand in the First-Floor main hallway in disbelief at what's happening to the school. I'm glad Maggie and Ricky didn't witness this.

For the past few months, I've taken many trips around the halls, never knowing which will be the last before Mulberry School succumbs to the wrecking ball, which looks to be very soon now. If I could cry, I would as I'm watching Mulberry being torn down after 85 years.

I walk into the gym. There's clutter by the stage, which is being torn up. I "met" ol' Ricky there before he was aware of me. There's nothing left there, so I go to the north hallway and step into a couple of classrooms. In one, students have written their names on the chalkboard, one with the date next to her name, "10/19/02." Back to the main hallway, I look into the now empty principal's office. It still looks strange to see it empty with clutter on the floor, much like when it was built so long ago.

I go to the south hall and walk toward the southeast stairway. Just beyond the locker rooms is a gaping crack in the floor, hazardous for a human to cross. It appears to be where the 'new' east addition was added in 1950, and that section of the school has been pulling away. I continue on to the southeast stairway and the exit. Over the past few months, kids have entered the building past the "keep out" signs and written graffiti on the walls and surviving chalkboards. There's a board leaning against the wall next to the southeast stairway. An empty white plastic jug sits next to it with other discarded clutter. A distraught student has written on the board:

> *We hate you; this is our school; don't tear it down! Our memories won't keep out!*
> *Class of '08.*

I, too, worry about the memories that might end up as dead as I am. What are they thinking? History is priceless. No amount of money can buy it or the memories that go with a building. Why not tear the east end off and shore up the rest as you seal off that end. That's a better way.

I go back to the main hallway and look for my "void spot." It's still there and I step onto it. Nothing around me now.

"Do you have a question?" it says.

"I'm losing the school. What do I do?"

"You've moved before."

"From here to here," I say, "but where to now?"

"There should be an option or two out there. And there's one not far from here."

"Either Random or Northside?" I ask.

"Both will face Mulberry's fate sometime."

"Then where?"

"How about Tonovey School building," it says.

"Maybe so," I say.

"Although you might have competition," it says.

About the author

Eric T. Reynolds is Editor/Publisher with Hadley Rille Books (hrbpress.com). He was born in the Flint Hills town, Eureka, Kansas, has also lived elsewhere in Kansas, and on the US East Coast. His fiction has appeared in the magazines *Mythic Circle, Galaxy's Edge,* in *Sci Phi Journal,* and in several indie press anthologies, and he had several non-fiction science articles published in an encyclopedia about the history of space exploration. *The Legend of Mulberry School* is his third novel. His first two novels, *The Artifacts* and *The Road to Sugar Loaf.* Contact him at erictreynolds@gmail.com and on Facebook as Eric T. Reynolds and his website:

erictreynolds.com

Acknowledgments

Special thanks to my first readers Debra Carbaugh Robinson and Sherry Stapleford, both of whom allowed me to bounce ideas around as I went through the process of creating the first draft. And to Nancy Reynolds who read the partially edited version to confirm the good and the bad. And to my editors, Laura Ripper and Rose Reynolds who found the best ways to make the final version better.

I also appreciate the assistance of the Greenwood County Historical Society in my research of the final days of Eastside Grade School. Additionally, the Kansas Historical Society, kshs.org, provided invaluable free access to newspapers.com (for any Kansas resident to Kansas newspapers) through which I could search early 1900s issues of the Eureka-based *Eureka Herald* and *Democratic Messenger* newspapers, and the Library of Congress access to early 1900s issues of the *Topeka Capital-Journal* newspaper. I also received good advice and much encouragement and info from friends on the "You know you're from Eureka, KS when......" Facebook page.

People and Places

The following were actual *places* and **persons** who lived and worked in Eureka during the years this novel is set.

Eastside Grade School, North. Mulberry Street, 1873-1917.

Mulberry School – N. Mulberry Street, 1918-2003.

Lydia Thrall – Owner of the *Oxford Rooming Home*, 1914-1920s.

Principal Nibert, Principal, *Mulberry School*, 1918-1919.

W. D. Ross, Kansas State Superintendent of Public Instruction, 1913-1919.

Mary Service, Principal, *Eastside School*, 1913, and Greenwood County Superintendent, 1914-1917.

Julia Gould – Grade School Teacher, *Eastside School*.

Lewis Mueller – Contractor, the new *Mulberry School*. Constructed June 1917-March 1918.

West 3rd Grocery, **Ira Mack**, owner.

Royal Café – Main Street, **Mr. Gray**, owner.

Reuben Snyder – Good student, a well-liked young man who died in November 1918 at 14 years old from an injury in a football game between Eureka and Burlington.

Frank H. Brooks Clothing Store 100 block of North Main Street.

The Opera House Building – built 1884, building still viable.

Greenwood County Courthouse, Main Street, built 1873, French Renaissance style, designed by John G. Haskell (who also designed the Chase County Courthouse). Building was razed in 1955 and replaced with a newer courthouse due to structural concerns. (Note: the 1956 courthouse is a preserved example of "1950s modern" architecture.).

Citizens National Bank– 3rd and Main Street.

Home National Bank 200 Block, North Main Street.

Greenwood Hotel – 3rd and Main Street, built 1882. Renovated to current Spanish Mission Revival style in the 1920s. Building still used and viable.

Congregational Church – 3rd and Elm Streets.

Eureka Lumber Company on 3rd Street, later, the Houston Lumber Company.

Clark's Drug Store - 200 Block, North Main Street, later was a Rexall until perhaps the early 2000s.

Eureka Electric & Ice store – 100 Block, North Main Street

Eureka Post Office – Across the street from the back of the courthouse.